He didn't seem dangerous, just dangerously attractive

"You have no business being a criminal," Janet lectured.

For some reason her handsome intruder found Janet's remark very funny. "Does anyone?" Adam asked.

"No, but you can do better. I can tell just by looking at you . . . and wipe that smile off your face." Adam's grin was annoying and confusing.

"I am being serious," Adam replied evenly, his eyes still crinkling. "If you'll just let me explain . . ."

"Don't give me any song and dance. I caught you," Janet snapped back. "Now, I'll give you a choice. Either you agree to professional counseling or I call the police."

"Counseling!"

"Yes, I'd like to make you a test case."

Even as she said the words, Janet knew that in this particular case the real test would be to hold on to her heart.

Dixie McKeone, when she isn't writing romances and mysteries, can be found designing subdivisions and streets. Her background includes twelve years in civil engineering and surveying, and she has worked on designs for bridges, superhighways and dams. Her vivid imagination, combined with her unique background and experiences, brings a freshness, an edge of excitement to her writing. She has two grown daughters and lives in La Mesa, California.

Exclusive Contract

Dixie McKeone

Harlequin Books

TORONTO • NEW YORK • LONDON
AMSTERDAM • PARIS • SYDNEY • HAMBURG
STOCKHOLM • ATHENS • TOKYO • MILAN

Original hardcover edition published in 1986
by Mills & Boon Limited

ISBN 0-373-02867-9

Harlequin Romance first edition October 1987

To Mike Smith
To the counsellors of
Eclectic Communications
And to those everywhere who
work for the restoration of
interrupted lives.

Printed in U.S.A.

CHAPTER ONE

JANET TALBOT closed the front door of the house on Bayview Drive and with a sigh dropped her handbag and keys on the table in the entrance hall. The gesture was a statement. The nerve-racking experience of the first day on a new job was over. The next—she consulted her watch—fifteen and a half hours were hers to rest, to reflect on being all thumbs in her nervousness, and to build her strength for her second day as a counsellor in Venetia House.

As the name Venetia House implied, it was a residence, a temporary home for newly released inmates of the federal prison, where the counsellors and residents together worked to rebuild the interrupted lives.

She had made her statement in dropping her handbag and keys, but once she had closed and latched the front door she turned to pick them up again and noticed her reflection in the mirror. *Good grief* ! she thought as she stared at her reflection and moved quickly away. The zombie creature staring back at her wasn't Janet Talbot of Spencer, Iowa.

She told herself that vanity was bad for the complexion of her personality, but she still couldn't stand that reflection, gaunt from fatigue and the tension of the first day on the job, eyes too large as if she expected some horror to jump out from behind the table and eat her. She wondered if she had smiled once that day. They probably thought she was hiding tea-stained teeth.

All in all, she'd made a great first impression.

She removed the pins from her dark blonde hair and let it fall, shaking it out. Better, she thought. Less professional-looking, but at least she didn't look like a staring skeleton. No one should drive thirteen hundred miles and start a new job the day after arriving. Particularly when the job was the first in her career.

At least she'd been spared the problem of finding a place to stay when she arrived in town. She would be house-sitting for the next three weeks while Harry Binns was on a camping trip in Canada's north woods. Though she didn't remember him, Harry had grown up in Hartley, some fifteen miles from Spencer. Their mothers, meeting on an inter-county church committee, had ended a gossip session by solving their offspring's immediate difficulties.

Harry's note was still on the table, the corner of several sheets of paper just visible beneath her handbag. It had begun *For the next three weeks, my house is your house, and thanks for coming.* Beneath that gracious beginning, Harry had made a list entitled *Things you should know*, which included such items as that the switch to turn on the light in the garage was over the sink and not by the door where one would expect it, the handle of the commode in the small bathroom had to be jiggled to stop the water from running, and the intruder alarm system was out of order.

His attitude in his note had made it seem as if the favour was entirely on her part, but she felt that having a place to live more than turned the tables. But his house wasn't home. It was too modern and too large for Janet's comfort. A non-lived-in neatness in most of the rooms bothered her. Apparently Harry limited his use of the house to his bedroom, the kitchen, and the large family room at the rear of the house.

Her handbag and the large suitcase she'd left in the front hall were the only signs of occupancy. Janet picked up her bag and carried it to the guest room, where she scrabbled in a suitcase for a pair of jeans. Her hand closed on cold steel and she pulled out a Colt .38 automatic enclosed in a large, clear plastic bag.

'Mother!' she complained to a woman thirteen hundred miles away. Her mother had insisted that all big cities were full of crime amd she should have protection. Some protection, Janet thought. With her sense of order, she'd end up hiding it in the kitchen cabinets behind the soup plates and be two hours looking for it. Burglars would have to make an appointment if the gun were to do her any good.

She started to shove it back beneath the clothing, and then remembered that in Harry's list of *Things you should know* he'd mentioned the failure in the burglar alarm system. She reluctantly placed the gun on the night-stand. She would need to make a decision, either to register it or send it back to Iowa. But not just then, she was too tired. She'd put off her apartment-hunting for a couple of days, she decided. She was just too tired. Instead of changing into her jeans, she found her pyjamas and changed out of her dress. She'd eat something, relax for a few minutes and go to bed.

In the kitchen she opened the refrigerator, but nothing she had purchased the evening before looked interesting. She poured out a glass of milk and carried it into the den. 'Den' wasn't exactly the right word for the large, partially glassed-in room. In an alcove off to the side, and overlooked by a smaller window, a desk and a drafting table took most of the space, but the main part of the room was dominated by a huge russet velveteen pit sofa. The massive island of furniture was, Janet thought, about nine feet square, yet it sat diagonally in the centre of the room. Two sides were backed, and the rest of the space was filled with ottomans.

Not quite sure how to sit on it, Janet perched on one

edge and put her glass of milk down on the long table that flanked the back of the sofa.

She was wondering if she could find a news programme on the television when she wrinkled her nose at the odour of stale tobacco. Harry had left several pipes in the ashtray on his desk, and most of them were full of ashes. By tapping them on the edge of the ashtray, she emptied out the stale tobacco, dumped the ashtray in the kitchen, and stored the pipes in the drawer. But the odour still clung to the room.

Outside a stiff breeze was tossing the green puffs of the eucalyptus trees and she opened the patio door, intending to air the room. Then she saw her mistake. The drafting table was littered with plan sheets which, caught by the breeze, sailed out across the room. In a mad scramble, she gathered them and carried them back to the table, wondering how to weight them down.

Next to the desk she noticed a white plastic bin. In it were approximately a dozen large rolls of plans, each with a carefully lettered job name.

She'd roll them up, she decided. If left out, they'd gather dust and be soiled by the time Harry returned. It seemed little enough to do. She picked up a pencil and printed a label in a copy of the stylised lettering used by her host. Then, opening the large shallow drawer of the drafting table, she took out a manila file folder and swept into it the stack of 81/2 x 11 sheets of neat computations. She put it in the drawer along with a three-sided architectural scale and several triangles and pencils.

Once the table was clean, she returned to the comfortable sofa and picked up her glass of milk. Her view through the patio door was a panorama of San Diego's steep and heavily built-up hillsides. But Janet's eyes kept straying back to the sturdy, graceless oak drafting table. She envied Harry that table. Its sturdiness spoke of confidence and success. Obviously, Harry had both. He was a partner in a large, prosperous architectural and engineering firm and the house, its size and location, shouted financial rewards and success.

Success held a special connotation for Janet, synonomous with accomplishment. Her success might never be as spectacular as a modern building, she thought, but for her it would be more rewarding.

Still gazing at the drafting table, she visualised Harry's company, seeing it as a well-oiled machine, grinding out one success after another. Her imagery gave her confidence, a determination to rival that machine in her own small way. She finished her milk, carried her glass to the kitchen and washed it, and while the sun was still shining on San Diego she went to bed.

Earlier that day, Adam Richfield also thought of Associated Architects and Engineers as a well-oiled machine. At one o'clock he strode through the rear door of the company, slowing his pace as he walked up the long hall.

Then he stopped.

Leaning one broad shoulder against the wall, he savoured the atmosphere, the hum of the air-conditioning, the sudden burst of sound coming through the closed doors and the wall on which he leaned. He was home, surrounded by his 'family'.

Home and family was the company and his employees, so each morning, after a shower and a shave, he drove to the office. As he listened to the noise, the fatigue lines eased in his craggy, deeply tanned face.

His eyes, a startling blue against the deep tan, narrowed in amusement as he heard a clatter from the room behind the wall, followed by some ribald comment he didn't quite catch. He enjoyed the laughter as much as if he'd heard the joke. He'd been away too long, he thought. But the job in Texas was a multi-million-dollar project. When Jim Kerns, the most experienced of the company's construction engineers, had broken his leg, Adam had been unwilling to trust the project to a new employee. So leaving the company in the hands of Harry Binns, his junior partner, Adam had flown to Texas himself to oversee the job until Jim was able to take it over.

Adam hadn't worried about the company. His and Harry's people were the best. But he missed them. He was glad to be back, and glad he had made it back in time for Harry to take his camping trip. Adam had had a vacation last year. Harry had not.

Across the hall from where Adam stood was total silence. But every desk was in use. Adam never understood how architects could be so quiet. But they were Harry's bailiwick. The wall he leaned against sheltered 'his' department—civil engineering—geometric bedlam.

While he listened, he heard an outraged voice and several shouts of laughter. A stranger would wonder how the people in that room accomplished anything, but Adam's people always came through, even when the job seemed impossible.

He continued up the hall, told Jenny, the secretary, he'd arrived, and went into his office, idly flipping through the day's mail while he waited. Before long they'd come trooping in, the department heads with the little problems too minor to drop on him during his daily telephone calls from Texas. An engineer would want to switch his vacation. Rhoda Manion, his project manager, would probably want some bright trainee to have a sudden and unexpected raise in salary.

He didn't expect the Wainwright problem.

'Boss!' Rhoda exploded as she bounced into his

office, the rolls of the good life, as she called her excess weight, bouncing as she hurried across the floor and gave him a brief hug. 'I've missed you! You should have been here for the Perkins Jubilee!'

'Dammit! I don't hug surveyors,' Adam complained after the fact. He playfully pushed her away.

He made a fast mental comparison between the company projects and Rhoda's name for the job, assuming she was referring to the South Bay Center. He believed the owner was Perkins. His project engineer's vocabulary consisted mostly of ambiguous nicknames. She was, at times, confusing, but she possesed an almost infallible talent for scheduling different parts of a job so that they meshed. She was also an excellent surveyor and a close friend.

'Okay, what have you been doing?' he asked as he sat down behind his desk. 'I suppose you've ruined the company and we'll be ten years in hock?' He paused and looked down at his watch. 'Maybe only five years. You've only had half a day.'

'Yep!' Rhoda agreed, and dropped into the chair across his desk.

Adam hadn't missed the fact that she was carrying the battered shorthand pad she kept on her desk to make notes of issues to be brought into his office. But before she could flip to the proper page, the door opened again and Norman Edwards looked in.

'Welcome back, Boss. Hope you had a nice trip,' he said, his voice preoccupied, and his gaze turned back to Rhoda. 'Manion, have you got a minute?'

Adam expected Rhoda to lay a list of small problems on him, and he had pulled forward a yellow legal pad and picked up a pencil. But Norman's sudden intrusion, his preoccupation, and his use of Rhoda's last name, put him on the alert. He pushed the pad aside and dropped the pencil on it. In the shorthand of the office, use of last names among the employees was a flag saying 'No time for games'.

'What is it?' Adam demanded.

'I don't think it's anything,' said Norman, shifting slightly. 'I was just wondering if Rhoda had the Wainwright plans.'

Rhoda moved in her chair and turned to look at the project manager of the architectural department. 'On Friday you said they were all set.'

Norman's boyish face, an incongruity under the hair that was turning slightly silver, scrunched into lines of thought. 'That's what Harry said. I'm sure they're okay. I just can't find them.'

'Oh, damn,' muttered Rhoda. 'We've got to have them by four.'

'What's the rush?' Adam asked.

Wordlessly, Rhoda pointed to the appointment calendar on his desk, and he saw he was scheduled for a meeting with George Wainwright the following morning.

The man was a pain in the neck! He was one of the company's best clients, his jobs were the big money-makers that had helped Associated to grow, but the game had to be played exactly according to his rules. A major developer out of Colorado, his usual tactic was to give the company twenty-four hours' notice and then fly in to check on the progress of a design, and he had an irritating tendency to think every job should proceed with twice-human speed. Adam could handle the man's impatience, but he'd be on a bad footing if they couldn't find the plans. Still, at the moment he wasn't worried.

'They must be here,' he said. 'Rhoda, check your file. Maybe the architectural sheets were put in with the site plans.'

She nodded, left the shorthand pad lying on his desk, and followed Norman Edwards out of the office.

When the door closed Adam sat for a moment, then got up and walked back into the hall. Halfway down the corridor he turned into the employees' lounge, where some brightly painted wicker furniture clustered at one end. At the other, a big round formica table was surrounded by eight metal dining-chairs, and in one corner the tall cylindrical tank of a commercial coffee pot held court among the containers of powdered cream and real and artificial sugar. On the wall shallow narrow shelves held an odd assortment of personal coffee cups.

Adam turned the handles on two large white mugs before he found the one proclaiming in bold black letters, 'The Boss'.

He filled his cup and stepped back out into the hall, listening to the voices coming from the architectural and engineering departments. In ordinary times the doors leading into the main passageway through the building were kept closed. Now they stood open and Norman Edwards' voice drifted to him as the architectural project manager instructed a draftsman to search for the Wainwright plans in likely places. Rhoda's more strident voice was also issuing orders. Adam shrugged and went back to his office. They'd find the plan sheets, he decided.

Back at his desk, he finished flipping through the mail, pushed the engineering and architectural magazines to one side to be read later, and came upon a folder someone had thoughtfully marked 'Rubbish'.

An apt term, he thought as he flipped through it. He scanned a letter from an insurance company that suggested the company could have twice the medical benefits at half the price, and an advertisement from a commercial painter that could promise him a bargain on repainting the office. He wondered if he should consider it, and made a mental note to take another look at the overall condition of the building. He'd have to depend on Rhoda for an answer, he thought. While he was at it, maybe he should get her over to his apartment for an opinion on what he should do to make his place seem more like a home. He knew it lacked something, but he was impatient with little household details. And the women he'd been dating recently didn't seem the type to help him out. He'd rather have Rhoda's opinion than anyone else's, he thought. Her place had a comfortable feeling about it, and a little dash of style. Her husband George always seemed at ease there—when he wasn't running round the world putting in oil wells.

The idea of asking Rhoda for advice bothered Adam slightly. In the past year he had dated a lot of women, but he immediately rejected all of them in favour of getting Rhoda's assistance when it came to something as important as his comfort. He wondered why. Just asking himself that question should tell him something about his life, he decided. But it was an unsettling thought and he pushed it away. Time to think about that later.

A stack of pink 'While you were out' slips had been paper-clipped, probably by Jenny, the new secretary, and when finished with the 'Rubbish' file he flipped through them. No emergencies—mostly personal messages—anything needing immediate attention had been handled by Harry or Rhoda or the messages passed to him by phone while he had been in Texas.

He spent the next forty-five minutes checking through the accumulation, familiarising himself with the details on some new job. Then, wanting to know the full picture, he reached over to the corner of his desk and picked up Rhoda's shorthand pad. As he expected, most of her questions were more to the point than the advertisements that had been tucked in the file for him to see. And sure enough, her fourth note had been a question of giving a new employee a raise.

Ames, a rank beginner, hired two weeks before Adam had left for Texas, had been studying in his off-hours. He'd taken a drafting class at a local school, and had become a great deal more valuable in a short time than would have been expected from a trainee.

Rhoda, who had begun in the same position herself, was careful to notice improvements in new employees. Should he set a policy about raises and bonuses? Adam wondered. But he didn't have time to make a decision.

His door opened again and, shoulder to shoulder, Norman and Rhoda strode into his office and stood in front of his desk. By their expressions, Adam didn't have to ask—they hadn't found the Wainwright plans.

He felt his temper building and stifled it. No matter who was to blame, Norman and Rhoda weren't directly responsible. But it would be damned embarrassing if George Wainwright walked into the office and the plans for his job were missing. That didn't happen in Associated Architects and Engineers. It didn't happen to an important client like Wainwright, or to the home owner who wanted a small survey to locate his fence. A.A. & E. treated their clients with more respect.

'Where the hell are they?' he demanded, not expecting an answer and surprised when he got one.

'We think Harry took them home,' said Rhoda, causing Norman to shift uneasily and take a slightly defensive position. As senior member of the firm, Adam was referred to by both the engineering and architectural departments as 'Boss', but the architectural people were as loyal to Harry as Adam's engineers were to him.

'He wanted to double-check that job before he left,' Norman told him, a slight belligerency in his explanation.

'The idiot!' Adam half-chuckled, glad they'd at least

located the plans. 'Let's have a look in his desk and see if there's an extra house key in it.'

There was no key in Harry's desk. They found a box of keys in a secretary's desk, but they belonged to the company vehicles and the office. If Harry had a personal telephone directory listing any friends who might be looking after his place, he'd taken it with him. Though Adam and Harry worked well together and trusted each other in business, they weren't close on a personal basis. Harry always kept his private life private.

Adam's relief was evaporating. He was getting worried.

'You'd think he'd leave a set of keys somewhere in case he lost the ones he carried,' he grumbled.

'I never thought he'd be the flowerpot type,' murmured Rhoda.

Adam's brows snapped down as he threw an intense look at his project manager. 'You mean hiding the keys somewhere around the house?'

Rhoda nodded, but the motion of her head was not as emphatic as Norman's.

'A lot of people do,' he said.

Adam pushed back the executive desk chair with so much force that it bumped into the cupboard behind him. 'Let's get out there and take a look,' he said. 'We'll all go. It'll make the search faster.'

But no more productive. Harry didn't have flowerpots—at least not outside the house.

Rhoda's idea of checking any ledges within the reach of a tall man was a good one, but the Spanish motif and the columned arches that held the overhanging roof were smooth and left no place to hide a key.

'Then all we can do,' said Norman, his voice low with caution and worry, 'is to break into the house.'

'And get arrested!' Adam retorted.

He had to have those plans, but there was usually a relatively simple way of getting any job done if it was given sufficient thought. Since the office was not too far away, they decided to return and think over the situation, and possibly they'd come up with an answer.

Adam had driven about half the distance when he spotted a possible solution. Two police cars sat in a parking lot of a restaurant. Adam pulled in and parked beside them.

'Hey, good going!' Rhoda commented when she noticed the official cars. 'Burglary with escort.'

'That's what I'm hoping for,' Adam said.

And with Rhoda and Norman following, he strolled into the restaurant, waved away the hostess who would have escorted them to a table, and strode up to a booth where two uniformed officers were having pie and coffee.

Adam introduced himself and remained standing while he gave them a short explanation of his problem. But when he requested their assistance in getting into Harry's house, they turned sceptical.

'Housebreaking is a felony,' said the young ginger-haired and moustached officer, whose name tag declared him as Patrolman Brown. 'That's particularly true if anyone in the house is threatened,' he continued.

Rhoda, who had remained slightly behind Adam, stepped up by his side. 'If there was anyone *in* the house, we wouldn't need to play burglar,' she reminded them. 'If Harry was here, he'd bring the plans into the office.'

Officer Zolinsky, by his name tag, nodded sympathetically but seemed no more willing. 'You *think* the plans are there. What if they're not?'

'There's no where else they could be!' Adam snapped, and as the cops' eyes riveted on him he made an effort to control himself. 'They're not something Harry would take on a camping trip.'

'They could be in his car,' Officer Zolinsky suggested. 'Did he drive on his vacation?'

'No. He flew,' Norman spoke up.

'But are you sure he didn't leave them in the car?' Brown asked.

Adam, Rhoda and Norman exchanged glances. They had their opinions, but they couldn't swear to them as fact. Nor did they know what Harry had done with his car.

'Okay,' Zolinsky pushed the coffee cup away. 'You can't actually know the plans are in the house, so here's the situation. If we went in with you—if you got into the house and found the plans, you'd have legal justification, there would be no crime——'

'But if they're *not* there,' Officer Brown took up the explanation, 'then we'd have assisted you to commit an illegal act, and you're no less guilty because we were along.'

'You're saying you'd be considered accessories,' Adam stated the situation with fewer words. 'That could make an interesting trial.'

Both officers nodded and grinned a little ruefully. But Zolinsky, more sympathetic of their situation from the beginning, brightened with an idea.

'A judge might give you a court order. Then you'd be okay whether the plans were there or not.

Adam didn't have time for a court order. But he didn't want to leave the two patrolman with the feeling that they should keep an eye on Harry's house. Not that he'd said where it was, but he'd given them the general location.

He tried to appear receptive to the suggestion. 'Thanks! That's a good idea,' he said, offering his hand to each officer and ignoring the objections in the eyes of Rhoda and Norman.

On the way back to the office, both of them

questioned him about trying to see a judge.

'Forget it!' snapped Adam. 'It's already——' he glanced down at his watch, '——twenty minutes after five. There's no way we could get legal help this afternoon. And we've got to have those plans tonight.'

Then another complication occurred to him, and he swore. 'We can't get into Harry's house. He's got a security system.'

'But it's not working,' Norman spoke up with his first real enthusiasm of the day. 'I heard him on the phone, not long before he left. They need a couple of weeks to get some gizmo that went out.'

'What kind?' demanded Rhoda. 'They don't come with gears.'

'*I* don't know! Something to do with the garage door,' Norman answered. 'Anyway, the main thing is, we don't have to fight a burglar alarm.'

'Well, that settles it,' Rhoda said. 'It looks as though we do the dirty deed after all.'

Back in the office, they struggled with cups of thick coffee, the residue of the big pot, and finally gave it up as they made their plans to carry out what Rhoda had nicknamed 'The Wainwright Caper'.

'I don't have any black pants,' Norman was objecting.

'Jeans are dark enough,' Rhoda was saying. 'But you've got to wear a dark top too. You can't go slipping through the bushes in a white shirt.'

'Okay, here's the way I see it,' said Adam. He'd been ignoring the chatter between Rhoda and Norman while he visualised Harry's house and tried to remember how much shrubbery was available for cover. He was familiar with the inside of the house. For three months, while they searched for affordable office space, they had run the company from Harry's den.

'I'll have to wait until after it's fully dark. Then I'll go in, get the plans, and you two wait here. We'll make any necessary corrections tonight. The prints can be run first thing in the morning.'

'You're not going over there by yourself,' Rhoda said.

Norman, never as outwardly energetic as his engineering peer, slid forward on the chair and put his hands on his knees. 'You're not going by yourself, Boss,' he repeated Rhoda's sentiments. 'Someone has to be lookout while you're in the house.'

'And someone has to drive the car,' Rhoda added. 'Suppose a neighbour spots you? We may have to make a fast getaway.'

'Getaway, hell!' snapped Adam. 'If I can get into the house without any trouble, even if they do call the police, the plans are *there*! You heard the cops in the restaurant. Once I've got the plans in my hand, I've got legal justification.'

'And you'd be three days proving it,' said Rhoda. 'How will it look to Wainwright if he has to review his plans in jail?'

Adam couldn't help grinning. So long as Rhoda and Norman were outside, he wouldn't mind having them with him. He took most situations in his stride, but he'd never broken into a house or been in a position where he might have to face the law. And he wasn't particularly looking forward to it. If Rhoda and Norman remained outside, they'd be guilty of nothing more than trespassing, and he, as Harry's partner, would have justification.

Like Adam, Norman was single, and Rhoda's husband was off rooting for oil in South America. So the three went out to dinner and then spent the rest of the evening changing clothes and gathering burglar supplies.

'This mess looks like something out of a cartoon!' Adam complained as Rhoda brought her contributions—a wire coathanger, two sizes of paperclips, two sizes of hairgrips, and several large rubber bands.

But when he objected she held her ground. 'I'm telling you, Boss, you can do anything with a coathanger and a paperclip,' she said. 'And when they won't work, a hairgrip always does it!'

'But why rubber bands?' Norman wanted to know.

Rhoda shrugged. 'They're just handy.'

By the time they'd added several other items to the pile on Norman's desk, two small penlights and Norman's contribution of dark paper, Adam complained that he'd have to take an attaché case to carry everything.

'And why the paper?'

'You need light to pick a lock,' Norman explained, 'and if I'm with you and hold up a sheet of the dark paper, it'll shield what you're doing.'

'Might as well,' Adam was resigned. 'Maybe we should take a theodolite to survey the situation first.' His joke about a piece of surveying equipment brought censorious looks from his two assistants. 'And how do you pick a lock anyway?' he queried after they'd stowed the equipment in the attaché case and were driving out to Harry's neighbourhood.

Norman didn't have any suggestions.

'You just kind of put a wire in there and jiggle,' Rhoda offered.

'I'm not trying a door lock,' said Adam. 'Be easier to open a window—I think.'

But the window wouldn't co-operate either.

Rhoda was sitting in the car, around the corner. She had the window down, listening for any commotion, ready to make a dash to pick them up if they found themselves in trouble, but Adam refused to signal for assistance in breaking in.

While Norman held a penlight on the latch, and the

dark paper as a shield, Adam first tried a paperclip, but
though he could slip the wire in the casing, the metal
was too soft to move the lock. The wire of the
coathanger, when he'd fished it from the attaché case
and scattered the hairgrips, was too large in diameter to
slip in the narrow opening.

Without using more light than they could risk, they
couldn't find the hairgrips.

'Maybe people take courses in burglary,' muttered
Adam.

But Norman, frightened enough to be trembling,
threw his boss a scared look and didn't open his mouth.

'Well, when in doubt use a credit card,' Adam said,
and pulled out his wallet.

The latch gave with a soft snick, and Adam eased the
window open. Pulling back the curtains and using one
of the penlights, he checked for furniture in his path.

'Put the stuff back in the case,' he whispered to
Norman. 'When I find the plans, I'll hand them to you
through the window.'

'Aren't you coming back?' asked Norman, his voice
trembling, so low that it was practically inaudible.

'You take the plans to the car,' Adam repeated. 'I
can't come back out of the window. I've got to lock it
and go out of the front door. I can't leave Harry's house
open to thieves.'

Adam knew the layout of the house well enough to
know he had got into the family room, where Harry
kept his drafting table and desk. As he expected, he
found several sets of plans rolled up and tucked in a
large bin. The big receptacles were as much a part of an
architect's or engineer's furnishings as his pencil.

Adam was only seconds in finding the roll of plans
carefully labelled 'Royal Arms'. The lettering puzzled
him. Harry had not written the name on the roll. To a
layman, most architectural and engineering printing

looks alike, but to someone in the field each is as different as individual handwriting or fingerprints. Adam frowned, wondering who had made that label.

With a shrug he assumed it was probably the new secretary, Jenny. He picked up the roll and carried it back to the window.

Just as he was handing it out to Norman the back door of the house next door opened, throwing a beam of light across the lawn, and in its shaft they could see a small dog dash out on the porch and down the steps.

'Get out of here!' Adam told Norman.

There was no fence between the two yards. If the dog decided to come their way, he might raise a commotion when he found strangers wandering around after dark. Norman, with a panicked look in the dog's direction, decided to circle the house to prevent being discovered by the neighbour's pet.

Adam softly closed the window, latching it securely, and allowed the curtain to fall back in place. He waited a full two minutes before using his shielded penlight. He crossed the family room and entered the hall, but a couple of steps further on he quickly shut off the light. The arched and doorless entrance to the dining-room was outlined sharply, because the curtains in the front of the house had not been pulled. If a neighbour saw a light moving through Harry's house when he was on vacation, Adam would have a lot of explaining to do, explanations for which he didn't have time, and which he could no longer substantiate since he'd given Norman the plans.

He moved along in the semi-darkness, trusting his memory of his partner's home to guide him. But on none of his visits to Harry's had there been a suitcase in the hall. He tripped over it and fell headlong.

Before he could get to his feet, he was blinded momentarily as the hall lights flicked on. He sat up and looked behind him. His gaze met a pair of wide, deep grey eyes. A young woman stood in the hall wearing a pair of white ruffled shortie pyjamas. Her clothing was opaque enough for modesty, but its brevity gave him an excellent view of long slim legs. Beneath the fulness of the pyjama top, the swelling of her breasts caused the flounce to extend a gratifying distance beyond what appeared to be a slim waist and flat stomach. Her dark blond hair, pressed into waves as she had slept, framed an attractive face.

She was a vision only marred by the blue steel automatic, pointing at the exact centre of his chest.

CHAPTER TWO

JANET had been as blinded by the light as Adam, but with a willpower that surprised her she refused to blink. Any show of weakness might lead the intruder to attack. She stood perfectly still, aiming the barrel of the gun directly towards his chest and holding it with a steadiness born out of the knowledge that she could do very little harm with an unloaded weapon.

As far as she could tell, her burglar was unarmed and intimidated by the weapon in her hand. His gaze kept moving from her face to the weapon and back again. Afraid to trust her voice, she stood staring at him almost unblinking. The weapon never wavered.

What did she do now? she thought. The news was always full of people breaking in—of burglars and robberies—but it had never occurred to her that she might one day face an intruder.

She continued to stare at the man on the floor. He certainly didn't fit her vision of a burglar. She caught herself up. Her field training and education had taught her there was no 'type'. A burglar could be tall and rangy. The close-fitting turtlenecked sweater showed off a muscular chest and arms, and his jeans were stretched over thighs too well formed to call him lanky. There was a certain ruggedness about the man, a deep tan and the clear eye that spoke of a healthy life, and yet none of those facts automatically prevented him from being a burglar.

There was an air about him that warned 'dangerous when thwarted', but Janet wasn't sure the danger was physical. After his initial shock at seeing her, his look had become almost assessing, as if weighing her on a female scale. And his expression had begun to change; his eyes and the twist of his mouth lost the look of shock and took on a distinct irritation.

He'd make an interesting case, she thought as she continued to stare at him. He started to move, and still afraid to trust her voice Janet took half a step forward and put both hands on the gun. Her threatening gesture convinced him to remain where he was. But instead of seeming frightened—she had expected his eyes to shift, looking for a means of escape—he physically relaxed but continued to stare straight at her. A sigh, a hiss of irritation, whistled between his teeth.

'Have you been here all the time?' he demanded.

Janet blinked in surprise. He was the burglar! What right had he to ask questions of her? Still, sure that silence was her best defence, she said nothing. But though she still held the gun, he seemed no longer intimidated by it. He balled one fist and struck the suitcase in frustration, the muscles in his jaw working in anger.

'I don't believe this. I go to all this trouble and *you're* here!' The bright blue eyes sparkled with dagger thrust. He pointed an accusing finger at her as if she were a child being chastised. 'This house was supposed to be empty!'

'That's usually what a burglar hopes for when he breaks in,' Janet retorted.

She hadn't meant to speak. Her voice often gave away her emotions, and she was afraid he'd hear her trembling. But her remark had been as steady as her hand. Then she realised that she wasn't really afraid of this stranger. She should have been, she knew, but fear couldn't be turned on and off voluntarily. For some inexplicable reason, hers had left with his anger.

'Yeah, I'm after the Henry Mancini album collection,' he muttered. 'This is your suitcase? You picked a crazy place to leave it!'

'Sorry, I wasn't expecting company through the window,' Janet answered, thinking this conversation should be recorded for *Believe It or Not*. She supposed he had come in through the window. Wasn't that usual for burglars?

She almost forgot the gun. Her hand wavered from the weight, reminding her she held it, and she took a firmer grip. The renewed attention to her defence seemed to make him angry again.

'Either put that damned thing down or call the police,' he demanded. He reached for the handle of the suitcase and set the bag upright against the wall. Then he braced his hands on the floor. 'I'm getting up now,' he spoke with slow deliberation. 'I'm not coming within ten feet of you.'

'Stay where you are,' Janet heard the worried waver in her voice.

'Don't be stupid. If you're calling the police, you need to be where there's a telephone. If we're continuing this staring match, I want to sit on a chair and be civilised.'

Janet watched him warily as he rose slowly and turned his back on her, walking into the chrome and glass living-room. He'd bolt for the windows and escape, she thought. The tight jeans and dark blue turtleneck sweater showed every bulge of his muscles. He couldn't be taking away any of Harry's possessions. She'd be just as happy to see him go.

She edged along the far wall of the hallway, both hands on the gun as she kept him in sight. Instead of heading for the windows or the sofa in front of the fireplace, he went to the back wall and opened what she thought was a wall mirror, exposing a bar.

'Wait a minute,' Janet ordered. 'You can't just——' She bit her lip. None of her case histories or her field training had ever described anything even remotely resembling this encounter. She was a little afraid to give him orders. If he continued to ignore her, what could she do?

He mixed two Scotch and sodas. When he turned, she saw the first hesitancy in him since he'd overcome his feelings of intimidation over the gun. Still moving slowly, he strolled to a chair and put one glass down on the table beside it. Then he carried the other to the sofa, where he sat stretching his long legs in front of him.

When she remained in the doorway, he gestured impatiently towards the chair. 'If I were wearing that outfit I'd sit down,' he said shortly.

Janet looked down at her pyjamas and blushed, more with indignation than with embarrassment. 'My clothing is proper for sleeping! If it offends your sense of modesty, break in during the *day*!'

'Oh, I don't mind. The men in the neighbourhood don't either.' He waved a hand towards the window.

She had forgotten to draw the curtains. As she realised she was in full view of anyone passing on the street, her face grew hotter and she took a step backwards. Her first thought was to rush to her room for her robe. And leave a burglar sitting in the living-room? She hurried across the room and dropped into the chair.

'I went to bed before it was dark,' she explained. 'I didn't think of the curtains.' Why was she excusing herself to him? He was the criminal. She was in the right and had been trained to control the situations around her. Besides, she had the *gun*.

'My clothes are not the issue.' She clipped her words in her best schoolroom manner, determined to wipe that mocking look from his face. And in a spirit of bravado, she held the gun in one hand and picked up the drink in the other, taking a hefty swallow.

Dragon fuel! If she opened her mouth she'd ignite the

room! Whew! So that was Scotch whisky. The grimace that raised her eyebrows and twisted her mouth had begun in her stomach and worked its way up to her face.

'You'll get an extra five years for mixing that drink,' she gasped when she could speak again.

She wasn't sure whether the fire raging inside her was due to the liquor or his amusement. He wasn't getting away with it. She'd had enough of his managing.

'Are you ready for an explanation?' he asked, settling back on the sofa.

Either the whisky or his superior tone caused her to flare up. She forced herself to remember he was the criminal. The situation was under *her* control and she would handle it. Her training taught her to take a firm line until she had established the necessary rapport and then ease off into a positive reinforcement, but first she must set her control.

'I think I've heard all the explanations,' she snapped. In truth, she'd read more than she'd heard, but he didn't know her experience.

'All?' He raised his eyebrows.

'All,' Janet repeated. 'It was a mistake—I had a reason—I needed money for my family—my life is full of bad luck—you name it!'

Somewhere in her list, she'd struck a chord. His eyes flashed. 'None of those things could possibly be true?'

'Maybe,' Janet deliberately kept her voice crisp. 'But out of your mouth, they'd be lies and we both know it.'

'Oh?' His voice turned dangerous. 'You automatically know I'd tell a lie?'

'If I give you a chance.'

'Then why don't you call the cops and turn me in?'

'Because I have something else in mind for you.'

Her initial surprise was almost as great as his. But on reflection, she realised an idea had been taking shape in her mind for years. All her studies had been trained towards the rehabilitation of the convicted criminal. But if a lawbreaker could be helped before he was arrested, tried and convicted, it might be far easier to straighten out his life and much cheaper for society. At least he wouldn't be carrying the scars of prison life.

'Let me see your driver's licence,' she demanded.

Adam was surprised again. But after a speculating gaze he shrugged, twisted on the sofa, and pulled out a slim wallet from the back pocket of his jeans. As he started to hand it over, she shook her head.

'Just your driver's licence,' she said in the exact tones of the Nevada Highway Patrolman who'd stopped her for speeding. Hearing an authoritative voice couldn't hurt him.

He responded by removing a small rectangular card enclosed in a clear plastic case, and with an expert flick of the wrist sent it sailing across the intervening space between them.

Feeling the need of courage, she'd taken a second swallow of her drink, and her stomach was going through another recoil when the card sailed into her lap. She picked it up. Adam Richfield. Thirty-three years old, if her mental maths was correct. He appeared to be taller than the six feet and lighter in weight than the driver's licence implied. Either he'd lost weight or his muscles were as hard as a rock. Janet would have wagered on the latter. The face was the same, the sensuous mouth had a slightly arrogant curve though he wasn't smiling. The bright blue eyes overrode the rest of his rugged face and offered a challenge, as if daring anyone to question him.

Janet committed the name and address to memory and flipped the driver's licence back. Not as expert, she sent it sailing wide and he lunged halfway across the couch to catch it. While he replaced the licence and pocketed his wallet, she took another sip of her drink.

Artificial courage was her label for liquor. At the moment, she was in need of a little bravery.

'Okay,' he said. 'You've seen my driver's licence. What now? Are you willing to listen to me?'

'I think you've talked enough,' Janet said. The whisky was burning in her stomach and her confidence was returning. 'It's my turn. Do you want me to call the police?'

'Not especially.'

'Then be quiet. Don't try to fob any stories off on me and maybe I won't.' Explaining herself and her plans wasn't as easy as she thought. Stalling, she took another drink.

The first gulp must have cauterised her taste buds and the nerves in her throat. The drink went down more easily.

'You should be ashamed of yourself,' she said as she put the glass down. 'You've got no business being a criminal.'

For some reason, Adam found that remark funny. 'Does anyone?' he asked.

'No——' Janet answered slowly. After thinking about it, her censure of him didn't make much sense. 'Some people get themselves into such messes it's understandable. But you can do better! I can tell that just by looking at you—and *wipe that smile off your face, mister*!' she yelled as he seemed to be struggling to keep from laughing. 'Now either you take me seriously or there's no more to be said.'

'I'm serious,' said Adam, his mouth straight. His eyes were still crinkling.

'Okay,' said Janet, wondering why her voice seemed a bit husky. The liquor had roasted it, she decided, and made a note not to drink Scotch whisky again.

In as few words as possible, and most of those jumbled, she introduced herself and told him about her occupation. She even admitted to being new to the area and explained she was house-sitting. But because a counsellor needed to instil trust and confidence in the client, she omitted the fact that this was her first full-time job. Instead, she launched directly into the scheme she had in mind.

'You'd probably prefer to walk out of that door and go your own way without benefit of the authorities,' she said, wondering if her formality was born out of the Scotch. Well, it was British liquor and they were formal, weren't they? An idle tangent thought crept in. If she drank tequila, would she automatically know how to do the Mexican Hat Dance?

She shook her head, a sharp little snap, physically jerking her mind back to the subject.

'If you'll just listen to my explanation——' Adam Richfield was saying.

'Oh, stop it!' Janet's irritation whipped across the room. She took another sip of the drink. Not a big sip, she'd emptied the glass. Where did it all go? Why was she having such a hard time concentrating?

'Don't give me some song and dance,' she ordered him, *or let's switch to tequila*. This irrevelant little thought sneaked in, but she pushed it aside and stuck to the subject.

He was glowering at her, but she would not be bamboozled by an illegal intruder. 'Don't try any stupid excuses. I caught you. That's that!' She waved the gun for emphasis. She might as well, she decided. She couldn't seem to hold it steady any longer. 'I'm going to credit you with being man enough to stand up to what you've done. Maybe you're not man enough. Are you just a weasel ready to slide down any rathole just to get out?' Could a weasel slide down a rathole? she wondered. But that was too immaterial. She'd stung his male ego and he reacted.

Across the room, he seemed to widen as he leaned forward and started to rise. Either he was some rubber man or her focus was playing tricks.

'Don't threaten an occifer—an occi—an officer of the court!' she ordered. Strictly speaking, only her boss at Venitia House held that position, but she decided to stretch a point. Apparently she'd said the right thing, for he looked indecisive for a moment and then sat back. 'Now will you co-operate or not?' she asked.

He didn't move again, though he sat with tensed muscles, like a cat pounced to spring. 'Let's say I'll hear you out.'

'Do you have a record?' Janet asked.

'A great jazz collection.'

'If you refuse to take me seriously——'

'Okay, dammit! I don't have a record. I've never been in jail—but you're not going to believe that.'

'Yes, I think I do,' Janet said slowly. 'Prison leaves marks on people. They're not the same for everybody, but you don't appear to have any of those particular scars.'

'Thank you for noticing!' he said shortly.

'Okay,' she said, pulling herself back to her original idea and wondering why it was taking her so long to get to it. 'I'll give you a choice. I'll call the police or you can agree to private counselling——'

If she'd said a walk on the moon, he couldn't have looked more startled.

'Counselling,' she repeated after being pulled off-stride by his surprise. 'I'd like to make you a test case——'

'Well, you can like and be *damned*!' he snarled. 'If you think you're going to get me in somewhere testing my I.Q. and probing my psyche, you're out of your silly little mind. Call the cops!'

'When I said a test case, I didn't mean that type of

testing,' Janet snapped back. 'That's not what a counsellor does.'

'Exactly what do they do?' Adam eyed her with distrust.

She straightened her shoulders, justifiably proud of her occupation and feeling no need to make excuses for it. 'Essentially we help our clients begin new careers in lawful occupations that interest them. We help them find places for training. We teach them how to apply for the jobs they want. We help them get settled, locate places to live and set up their lives——' despite herself, she was reacting to the distrust she saw in his face '—and once they're living their own lives, we step aside and let them do it,' she finished in a rush.

'And you want to put me on the road to being a law-abiding citizen,' he was sarcastic, half humorous.

'If you don't think you could handle it, maybe I shouldn't make the effort,' Janet retorted. She was slamming his male ego every time she opened her mouth, she thought, which was against every principle of her type of counselling.

Yet with Adam Richfield, she had reason. Shocking him into creating a new life for himself would pay greater dividends than he could imagine, since he'd never been behind bars. That was the shock and the destruction of the human ego that her career was designed to reconstruct. And she justified herself in her actions with the knowledge that if she reached this man across the room, he might never suffer what many others did.

'Make your decision,' she said.

'You're blackmailing me,'

'Call it what you like,' Janet was not put off by his accusation. 'You have a choice.' She let her words hang. She was striving hard to establish an authority in the face of a poise and assurance that would daunt most people.

Instead of giving her an answer, he rose slowly from the sofa, glass in hand, and with a questioning raised eyebrow pointed to the empty glass on the table beside Janet. She picked it up and held it out at arm's length, deciding not to make an issue over his wanting another drink, since possibly if he mellowed she would achieve her result.

The end justified the means, she thought. Up to a certain point, she amended. As she leaned forward, the low scooped neck of her pyjama top gaped slightly. And since he hadn't taken the glass, she threw up her right hand in which she held the gun and felt the cold steel on her chest as she held the pyjama top in place.

His eyes had drawn her attention to the gaping pyjama top. But while his look had been appreciative, though she could hardly consider it more than cursory, his attention seemed for a moment riveted on the hand and the gun that was now preventing any unwanted exposure.

'Just fix the drinks,' she said, and waved her other hand imperiously, ordering him to take the glass.

As he moved round to the bar, Janet turned in her chair to watch him. Her head was still swimming with the first drink, but she was not so affected that she was willing to sit with her back to him and allow him to take her by surprise. He seemed to have no such qualms, and presented her a dark silhouette of a masculine figure as, with his back turned to her, he busied himself with the liquor bottles.

'Let me get this straight,' he said as he mixed the drinks. 'You want to choose an occupation for me, something lawful and——'

'No, no, you've got it wrong. I don't choose anything for you. You make your own decisions.'

'No aptitude tests? No I.Q. tests? I just say, I've always wanted to do this or that—and we go from there?'

'Within reason,' Janet said.

'You're putting limits on it. What kind of limits?'

'You can't say you want to be president of General Motors. You must start with something you're qualified to do or that a reasonable training will qualify you for, and work your way up.'

'But I choose the job,' Derek said thoughtfully.

'That's right,' said Janet. 'Then we work together on how to accomplish what you want. I'm a listening ear. I'm a backboard for you to bounce your ideas against, here to offer suggestions, to help you find opportunities you may not be aware of and help you to keep on the right track.'

The drinks made, he walked back round the chair and Janet watched him warily. But he stayed at arm's-length distance from the table as he put down her glass and then returned to the couch. Once seated, he raised his glass, and held it waiting for her to pick up hers. Obviously he was going to make a toast.

Seeing no reason to thwart it, Janet picked up her own drink.

'To blackmail,' he said, his blue eyes attempting to stare her down.

Knowing she was in the right, she met his eyes squarely and raised her glass another inch. 'To whatever it takes.' To prove she meant it, she took a large swallow of the drink, instinctively recoiling against the expected burn of the liquor. It wasn't as bad as she had expected. She had probably cauterised her insides with the first one.

'You actually think forcing me into this will work?' he asked.

Janet stared at the determined jaw and the glitter of

his bright blue eyes, and doubted it. She was facing a man with a great deal of determination, but if she could channel that indomitable will into a positive direction, she was sure he could be succussful at anything he tried.

'I think you could do almost anything you wanted to,' she told him, deciding now was the time to put forward some encouragement so necessary in helping people to rebuild their lives. 'I think you're a man who would inspire trust and confidence in people. You're articulate. You give the impression of being well educated. You're obviously strong and healthy.'

Her gaze slid down the length of his body as she made the statement, and by his flicker of a knowing smile it was clear he had noticed. To allow him to think her assessment was in any way personal was more than she could stand. 'And you might also consider this,' she went on hurriedly, as though her assessment of him physically had had a professional intent. 'You're not unattractive, though I will warn you women look for more in a man than just a good physical appearance.'

His smile turned to a smirk. 'I see. Am I to understand you think if I had a successful, law-abiding profession, I'd have more success with women?'

'Certainly,' Janet assured him.

'That's something to consider.' Adam turned thoughtful and picked up his glass again, finishing off his drink.

Across the room, Janet congratulated herself and reached for her own drink. She took careful aim and her two left hands picked up the two glasses. She eyed them thoughtfully, recognising in the doubling of her vision that the first drink had done considerably more damage than she'd expected. She resolved to take only the tiniest sip.

She put the glass down hurriedly as Adam Richfield rose from the couch. He stuffed his hands in his jeans' pockets and looked down at her.

'If I agree to your plan, am I free to go? No cops?'

She nodded emphatically. 'You give me your word that you'll call me within the next two days——' She paused, still having trouble thinking. 'I'll give you that long to consider what you think you'd like to do with your life. But after that, we'll make an appointment, we'll get to together in the evenings, and start putting your career together.'

'Two days,' Adam Richfield repeated.

'Will you give me your word?' Janet pressed.

For a moment he appeared as if he might say no, but then with a sigh he nodded in return. 'You've got it.'

'Then I'd appreciate it if you'd leave through the front door,' she said. 'It might be a novel experience.' She softened the remark with a smile and followed him into the hall, waiting while he removed the safety chain and turned the handle on the dead-bolt lock.

'Now I'll expect to hear from you,' she said. 'Remember I know your name and address.'

'Agreed.' He opened the door a fraction, then turned back to face her. 'Just one thing before I go,' he said, and with a sudden movement caught the wrist of her right hand that still held the gun. Holding it in a strong but not hurtful grip he twisted it slightly, so that both the handle and barrel of the weapon were horizontal.

He pointed to a button on the side of the barrel. 'The next time you hold a burglar at bay, take the safety off,' he advised. He released her arm, opened the door and walked out into the night, his dark hair and dark clothing soon blending into the shadows.

And Janet, after staring open-mouthed for a moment, quickly closed the door and leaned against it.

'Take the safety off,' she muttered, looking at the side of the gun. 'Why? It wasn't loaded anyway.'

Coming to herself, she relocked the door and walked

slowly back down the hall. She stood in the archway of the living-room, decided to leave the glasses where they were for the night, flipped off the light, and returned to her bedroom.

The bed seemed a little less stable than when she had lain down earlier that evening. Scotch whisky, she decided, was not for her. She made herself a promise that in the future, no matter how attractive a man was, she was not going to be bamboozled into drinking more than she should. But it was easy to understand how Adam Richfield could have that effect on a woman. He was a very attractive man. Dangerously attractive, she thought. She'd have to keep careful hold on her heart when she worked with this one. She could just imagine that a moonlit night, white wine and a good dinner could go to any woman's head if she sat across the table from Adam Richfield.

Dinner, she thought suddenly. That's why the Scotch had gone to her head. She hadn't had any. She should get up and eat something and counteract the effects of the alcohol. But it would be much nicer, she thought, stretching luxuriantly, to curl up and think about her plans for Adam Richfield.

Adam was late arriving at his office the next morning. His sleep had been disturbed by dreams of guns. His periods of wakefulness had been sharp-eyed with a growing anger.

The night before he'd run the gamut of too many emotions to settle deeply into any one. Fear, relief, anger, confusion and humour had all mixed together, surfacing and being replaced too rapidly to anchor on any particular feeling. But by the time he'd reached home his predominant emotion had been anger at being accused of being a thief. His wakefulness during the night had resulted in his oversleeping, and that hadn't helped his mood either.

So when he strode up the long hall of the office building the pounding of his heels indicated to anyone within hearing that the Boss was in a foul mood that morning.

Jenny, the secretary, took one look at his face and left her desk, hurrying down the hall. Adam had just hung up his jacket and walked over to his desk when she peeped round the corner of the door and entered with a cup of coffee.

'Thanks,' Adam bit off the word, not letting it linger a fraction of a second longer than was necessary. She was trying to placate his bad mood. He wasn't ready to let it go.

Jenny hadn't left the room before Norman and Rhoda entered, eyes alight with curiosity. But the perversity of Adam's attitude shelved their questions for a moment.

'What time is Wainwright coming?' he demanded as Rhoda, carrying her coffee cup, plopped into a chair.

Norman was making a job of closing the door. 'Next week,' he said at last, as he came over to sit by Rhoda.

'What?' Adam glowered. 'Did you mix the dates?'

'He called,' Rhoda broke in hastily. 'For some reason, he can't make it today.'

Adam, drumming a pencil on the pad in front of him, threw it down in disgust. 'Fine! I nearly end up in jail over that bozo and he's not coming!'

'Be glad, because we're not ready for him,' said Rhoda. 'After the mess last night, we didn't even get back to the office. And I want to know what happened. We waited, but you didn't come back to the car.'

'I thought you'd left,' Adam said. 'I walked home.'

Rhoda threw a dissatisfied look at her architectural peer. 'Norman went back and looked in the window. All I could get out of him was, "The girl, the gold gun, and everything".'

'And I mean "everything",' Norman nodded.

'That bitch!' Adam lashed out. But Norman's description had brought back the scene and he couldn't help a half-laugh.

'She didn't call the police?' Rhoda asked.

'No, she's going to rehabilitate me,' muttered Adam. His expresion dared Rhoda to laugh.

She accepted the challenge, her head thrown back in a guffaw.

'You mean you didn't explain what happened?' Norman asked.

'She wouldn't let me! She'd made up her mind. She wasn't about to be confused with facts. And you had the plans. I couldn't prove why I was there.'

'You seemed okay when I looked in the window,' said Norman. 'I mean, you were mixing drinks.'

'I got her bombed,' Adam smiled, remembering Janet's slurred speech, her confusion over her inebriated state, and her heroic attempts to keep to the subject. 'She didn't look as if she could handle a Scotch and soda.'

'How much soda?' demanded Rhoda, giving him a sharp look.

Adam's teeth gleamed white as he gave his project manager a grin. 'Very little. That was war.'

'Then you're going to see her again?' Norman asked. 'Some guys have all the luck!'

'What's she going to do to you?' Rhoda sat up, serious again.

Adam leaned back in his chair, and turning slightly sideways propped his feet on the corner of the desk. 'The idea seems to be to find me a job. I'm the executive type, you know,' he turned his eyes towards Rhoda. 'And if I had more to offer than just looks, I'd be modestly attractive to some women.'

Norman laughed.

Rhoda shook her head in wonder. 'There's no accounting for some female taste,' she said.

'Go sweep the back alley!' Adam swung his arm as if he was going to throw the pencil at her. If she'd been a man he would have told her to go to hell.

Norman turned serious. 'Well, now you can tell her the truth, and even if you don't we'll alibi you if she goes to the police. She can't prove you were ever there.'

Adam dropped his feet to the floor and sat up. The dangerous glitter in his eyes had set employees shaking in their shoes. 'Tell her nothing,' he growled. 'She called me a thief!'

'Boss,' Rhoda sounded cautious, 'don't rip her head off. She could have called the police.'

Adam ignored her, the anger building again.

'What are you going to do?' asked Norman.

'I don't know yet,' Adam's words came out from between clenched jaws. 'But she made a fool out of me, and the next round is mine.'

'Sorry, Boss, I don't think you're being fair,' Rhoda insisted. 'She caught you breaking into the house. What was she supposed to think? I mean, how often do good citizens go visiting friends who are on vacation and go in through the window?'

'I was willing to explain,' Adam said doggedly. 'I tried two or three times. I don't know what her hang-up was, but she wouldn't listen.'

'You didn't have to agree to be rehabilitated,' Rhoda argued back, her eyes crinkling with humour again.

'It was that or the cops. What would you have done?' Adam asked with a snap.

'Well, I don't see what you're so angry about,' Norman added his bit. 'Let's face it, that's one good-looking chick.'

But Adam's face, set in lines of anger, convinced the

two project managers not to push the situation any further. Remembering pressing matters in their departments, they left Adam to the solitude of his anger. But Norman had been closer to the truth than he knew.

In spite of the resentment that he harboured against Janet Talbot, Adam was well aware that she was an attractive woman. And he had asked himself several times during the night and once that morning whether her combination of feminine appeal and naïve enthusiasm hadn't been a deciding factor in his agreement to her scheme for his rehabilitation. But good-looking or not, she wasn't getting away with it. He'd made that decision and he'd stick to it. He'd given his word, and whether she believed it or not his word was worth something. But he wasn't going to let her put him in some training programme or send him out with his hat in his hand looking for a job.

Good God, he thought, what if one of his clients got wind of it? He needed an occupation she'd have to handle herself. What would it be? he wondered. What would make this little Miss Goody-Goody turn tail and run?

If the idea had hit him any harder, it would have knocked him off his chair.

He leaned back working out the details, part of his mind playing the devil's advocate so that the other half was ready with the answers to all her objections. He didn't want to wait a day to call her. He wanted to call her that afternoon, but perhaps he shouldn't be too hasty. Perhaps he should sleep on his plan. He wanted it to be perfect, because he was going to give Miss Janet Talbot a run for her money when it came to professions!

CHAPTER THREE

WHILE Adam was thinking of Janet and questioning himself on his motives, Janet was also engaged in some self-examination, hampered by a severe headache. Aspirin hadn't stopped the pounding in her head. She was experiencing her first hangover.

She also suspected Adam Richfield of recognising in her a lack of experience with liquor, and decided he'd used her ignorance to mellow her attitude towards him. Was alcohol responsible for her decision to work with him? she wondered. But she knew it wasn't.

The basic idea had occurred to her while doing fieldwork two years before. But would she have taken the risk if he hadn't been so attractive as he sat on the floor with a look of chagrin and outrage? She could see him again in her mind, his sparkling blue eyes showing disbelief that a *gun* could be pointed at *him*.

Maybe she wouldn't, she thought, and fairly admitted that his looks and attitude had a lot to do with her decision. While she didn't condemn the penal system as a whole, she knew some lives were wasted behind prison gates, and taking part of Adam Richfield's life would be a crime in itself.

Oops! Hold it, she warned herself. Her professionalism was bouncing around like a rubber ball. He was just another case. Since he wasn't a federal parolee, she'd have to limit her work with him to evening hours, and she'd limit her feelings too. She'd already learned that frustration and heartbreak could often be the result of getting too involved with a client, and resolved to tuck Adam Richfield away mentally until that evening. She pulled a stack of files towards her, consulted the note clipped to the first one, dialled a telephone number, and waited.

For the first week, Pete Hall, the director of Venitia House, had decreed that Janet would spend much of her time in clerical chores, one of which was to call different training programmes and verify the presence of their clients. He had explained, and Janet had agreed, that familiarising herself with the programmes and the opportunities available was a step towards her future assistance to the clients. It also gave her a chance to catch her breath and get to know her surroundings before plummeting headlong into counselling. As she worked, she made three sets of notes. One in a desk telephone directory, one on a shorthand pad in which she also inserted pamphlets advertising the services of their particular organisation or, when no pamphlets were available, handwritten notes from Pete Hall, and her third on a pad that would tuck neatly in her handbag. On the outside cover she had identified the reasons with the initials A.R. Even though she was too new on the job and in that area of the country to speak with any certainty on the success of any training programme or employment situation, she would have a starting point when she saw Adam Richfield again.

Throughout the day her list grew, and during the afternoon she was privileged to overhear a conversation between a client and a counsellor at another desk which proved the value of their work. Bob Chalmers, a red-haired, freckled-faced counsellor, sat listening to a chubby brunette as she described an insurance office where she was to start work on the following Monday. Both she and the counsellor were as excited as children. Already feeling a part of a job she had worked and studied for for years, Janet vicariously joined in the happy glow. She looked forward to the time when her first clients came in with solid assurance that they were putting their own lives back together. But she had her first client, she thought, her mind drifting back to Adam Richfield. Because that was what he was, though he might not be too happy about it and it certainly wasn't an official case.

Across the room, Bob Chalmers pulled out a file and made a note while the client watched, still almost bouncing on her chair in her excitement. He closed the file with a flourish and slammed his hand on it.

'The way you're going, Sarah, it won't be long before I shut this one for good.'

Janet, still watching and comparing the victory for Sarah with her thoughts on Adam Richfield, couldn't help but wonder if she'd be as enthusiastic when her work with him was finished. Certainly I will, she told herself. The statement was an emotional order, a decree. What good were counsellors if they held on to their clients? The object was to set them free to live their own lives once they had direction, purpose and confidence.

She jerked another stack of folders towards her and dialled another number, determined not to think of Adam Richfield again that day. She continued to give herself that order repeatedly during the afternoon and the evening. By eleven o'clock the next morning she was sure she would never hear from him again. He probably carried a phoney driver's licence, so there would be no point in contacting the police, she thought. And what if she did? What would she tell them? How could she tell them she waited two days before reporting a burglary because she wanted the burglar to come back? Her cheeks grew hot just thinking about it.

When she returned from lunch she found a note on her desk. *Pick you up at seven for dinner. A.R.*

Back at the Binns' house that evening, Janet carried

the large suitcase from the hallway, opened it, and
pulled out several dresses, eyeing with dissatisfaction
the wrinkles from packing. She knew she should just
choose one and press it, but her method of operation
when planning for an evening called for last-minute
decisions. She'd long ago learned to buy or work out the
proper accesories for each outfit and do it well in
advance. No matter what she planned, she never knew
what she was going to wear until she started her last
minute scramble.

'How can you be so organised in everything else and
get so flustered just going out for dinner?' Derek had
asked her.

Janet was bent over the suitcase in the act of getting
out a small jewel box, but even thinking of Derek
brought her up short, and she let her hands fall.

Derek Wells had been her second case when she was
doing her fieldwork. She had broken the first rule of
counselling. She became involved. More than just
caring deeply, she had let her heart become entangled
with the engaging car thief. Her rude awakening came
when he'd been arrested again. Not for one lapse, but
for a series of misadventures. She'd been ready to throw
over her career, sure she lacked the basic detachment
needed to become a counsellor. But luckily one of her
instructors had got the truth out of her. She was months
in accepting her involvement as a classic case of an
enthusiastic novice.

'They describe it in all the textbooks,' Dr Wilson had
said with a sympathetic smile.

'I guess when it happens you think you're different,'
Janet had replied. She still didn't see any similarity
between the warnings in the books and her own pain.

'We always feel we're unique,' the doctor had said.
His eyes had looked beyond her, back into a memory of
that 'we'. His expression, more than his words, had

helped Janet through the following months.

'And I won't get involved again,' she said aloud as she grabbed the jewel box and removed from it a black onyx necklace and earrings.

She picked up the black-and-white silk dress, slipped it on a hanger and carried it into the second bathroom. When the tub was half full of hot water, she hooked the hanger over the shower head so that the steam could pull out the wrinkles.

'I'm just going to work again,' she shouted to the empty house as she marched back to the bathroom she'd chosen for her own use.

Adam Richfield was just another client.

Using all the willpower she could muster, Janet held to her resolve through a lengthy invigorating bath and while she gave her hair another luxurious shampoo. Determined not to allow herself the time to fall back into indecision, she manicured her nails and, though bright red polish was fashionable and accepted for evening wear, she chose a clear pink tint, allowing the paleness of the perfect moons and the extension of the nails beyond her fingers to be identified as 'home-grown'.

Lacking her usual indecision and last-minute scramble, Janet was dressed, her black silk shawl folded neatly and laid with her evening bag on the table in the entrance hall, and she was scanning the classified ads for apartments when the doorbell rang. Catching up her bag and shawl on the way to the door, she opened it to find Adam Richfield standing on the narrow veranda that ran the length of the front of the house.

Dressed in a dark-blue silk suit, white shirt and dark tie, he was everything Janet believed he could be. But to see the transformation take place within forty-eight hours left her slightly stunned. She had been prepared to work for months. Seeing her widened eyes, he smiled, his white teeth gleaming, like his eyes startling against his deep tan.

'Arch-criminal number one reporting for rehabilitation,' he said. His eyes skimmed her briefly and he added, 'If I'd known parole officers looked like this, I would have turned myself in years ago.'

'Th-thank you,' stammered Janet, and struggled to regain her composure.

Stalling for time while her mind caught up with this unexpected development, she flicked open her bag, double-checked to make sure the house key was nesting in the bottom, set the lock on the door and then stepped out, closing it behind her. Possibly she'd been a bit too quick, she thought as she saw the slightest curl of a smile cross Adam's lips again. But if he intended to make a comment about her not having invited him in, he decided against it. Taking her arm, he led her up the walk.

The car waiting at the kerb was as elegant as his clothing. Janet was no expert on automobiles, but she doubted whether the vehicle could be more than a year old. And it was expensive, she thought, a Mercedes, definitely a sports coupé.

'Yours?' she asked, her eyebrows raised as she looked up at the man beside her.

His eyes flickered briefly. 'In a manner of speaking.'

Her mind had been on Derek earlier in the evening, and his penchant for driving and selling cars that didn't belong to him came immediately to mind. She didn't want to ask Adam Richfield if he was driving the car with the permission of the owner. To show a blatant distrust simply reinforced the negativity that drew the law-breaker further into crime.

But Adam Richfield had apparently understood her hesitation and knew it for what it was. 'It's rented,' he said shortly, and opened the door for her.

Feeling as though she had begun the evening on a bad footing, Janet knew better than to try to cover the situation with inane excuses. 'It matches the suit,' she said, smiling up at him.

He closed the door, and while he was walking round the back of the car, Janet bit her lip, warning herself that she was not behaving with the professionalism she'd spent years learning. She leaned back, forced herself to relax, and waited until he had started the car. They were driving down the street before she spoke again.

'I should have mentioned it before, but you took me by surprise,' she said conversationally. 'You look elegant tonight.'

His reaction was a bit unexpected as he tilted his head and looked down at his suit.

'That wasn't a crack,' she added hastily. 'Quite often we find clients feel insecure because they haven't learned to be comfortable in a suit and tie.'

Adam relaxed and gave her a half-smile and a shrug. 'Even I can't always walk round looking like a cat burglar.'

'Not many of my clients wear tailored suits,' Janet countered. 'Nor do they drive cars like this.'

Adam slowed the car as they passed two little boys on bicycles, then speeded up again when the children were safely behind them. 'Your people have been listening to the old adage that crime doesn't pay,' he said. 'They need to readjust their thinking.'

Janet gave him a sharp look. 'If it pays you this well, I wonder why you even listened to me.'

'Did you leave me much choice?' Adam slowed for a stop sign, started to proceed and then threw a glance at her. He brought the car to a full stop before crossing the street. 'Mustn't break the law with my parole officer in the car.'

'I'm not concerned with traffic tickets,' Janet answered.

She grabbed the edge of the seat as Adam drove across another intersection, and could have sworn he was taking them over a cliff. The car nosed over and on to a sharper downgrade than she'd ever imagined.

Used to the wide flat expanses of the mid-West, she gasped and looked at him wide-eyed. 'I thought they only had streets like this in San Francisco.'

'Oh, we have a few,' he said as they reached the bottom of the incline where the grade smoothed out again. 'Hills like this make some second-story work quite an effort.'

'The first thing we need to work on is your thought references,' said Janet. 'It's normal to think in reference of your previous experience, but now you're out to make a change. It would be far better if, once you decide on a new career, you consider what you see in terms of your new occupation.' She sounded just like one of her textbooks.

They were at the end of the street on which they'd been travelling. On the other side of the intersection, a walkway and verge was all that separated the street from the San Diego Bay. Close to the shore, small private pleasure boats were moored to the docks and further out, riding at anchor, larger pleasure boats and some smaller commercial craft rocked gently on the waves. Even further out, triangular white sails billowed, dipped and scudded along, the boats seeming to skim the water.

Janet felt as if her breath was being taken away by the motion. 'I feel as if I'm living in a postcard,' she said as the light changed and Adam turned the corner. 'Half the time I don't believe what I'm seeing.'

'Oh, you'll get used to it soon enough,' he said, his eyes on the traffic as he pulled into a faster moving lane.

Janet was slightly piqued that he didn't share her delight at the scenery. Feeling her own appreciation dimmed by his lack of enthusiastic response, she forced her mind to revert to the reason they were on their way out to dinner.

'Have you been thinking about a career?' she asked him.

'I've given it some thought.'

'Have you come to any decisions?' she pressed on.

'I know what I'd really like to do.'

'I'm anxious to hear what it is.'

The glance he threw her was a surprise. The last thing she would have expected of Adam Richfield was a sudden shyness, a self-deprecating smile and a hesitancy to talk. Two nights before she'd thought him a man of strong decision, of quick decisive movements. She would have said that once set upon a course, he would have moved ahead without the slightest self-doubt.

'Well, are you going to tell me?' she prompted since he hadn't spoken again.

He took a deep breath, gave her another look. From a lesser individual she would have interpreted his attitude as one completely lacking in confidence. He turned his eyes back to the road again.

'I'd hoped for a couple of drinks first,' he said. 'Something to build up my courage.'

But now he was speaking the language Janet understood. He was really no different from the clients at Venitia House, who without help were often afraid to make big changes in their lives for fear of rejection and failure.

'I can understand the worry over making a new move,' she said soothingly. 'I know it's an upsetting feeling. Remember, I've just made one myself. But I think you'll have much less to fear than you realise. Before long you'll probably be looking back on today and laughing at yourself.'

'You make it sound so simple,' he said. 'But remember you had the training for your job. You knew where you were going. I—I just don't know if I can handle it,' he went on. His shoulders seemed to slump, his tone more hesitant. 'It seemed like such a good idea today. I mean, I was still thinking about what you said the other night. That a person can do anything they want. I've thought about it for two days——'

'And now that you find that you have to admit your dreams to somebody, you begin to doubt them. Is that it?' Janet asked.

'More or less.'

'Remember that I told you that a certain amount of training is available.'

'Yes, but for how many occupations?' he said. 'I don't know what kind of schooling I could get. I know I'd have to have some help. Not that it'd need a full college course or anything like that.' He shrugged again, his shoulders drooping further. 'Maybe it was just a bad idea.'

'Well, I thought better of you than that,' said Janet, trying to push him into making some commitment, any commitment. 'How can I judge if you won't even tell me what it is?'

'Give me a little more time,' he said. 'After all, you sprang this on me all of a sudden. Your prisoners or patients or cases or whatever you call them——'

'Clients,' Janet corrected him.

'All right. Your clients have had some time to think about this. So far I haven't had quite forty-eight hours. Maybe you think it's easy just to pop out with a dream and risk somebody laughing at you.'

'But I won't laugh,' Janet said. 'That's the last thing in my mind.' She strove to find some way to make him feel more comfortable. 'I won't ask you to tell me right now what it is, but let's talk about it in general terms. That may make you feel better.'

He gave her a dubious look, but she continued undaunted.

'I take it we are discussing a lawful occupation?'

'Right.'

'Is it one you feel is within the limits of your basic education?'

He seemed to consider that a moment and then nodded.

'By the way, what is your basic education?'

'A smattering of college.'

Janet wasn't surprised, because she found him articulate and obviously intelligent, a man too intelligent to have chosen a career for which he was totally unsuited. But since he obviously wasn't ready to tell her what it was, she decided to tackle the the problem from a different direction.

'Do you mind if I ask some questions? Just general?' she asked.

As he shook his head, she pressed on.

'I won't ask you what it is at the moment, but let's look at it this way. What sort of training or experience have you had that makes you feel justified in attempting this dream of yours?'

'Well,' he said slowly, 'some knowledge of people, I guess, and I know the area.'

Janet was disappointed. Her first thought was that he planned to be a salesman—vacuum cleaners, encyclopaedias or insurance. Those jobs required patience, a virtue she thought lacking in him, though she was sure he'd have the tenacity for it.

'What additional training do you feel you'd need?' she asked, pressing on.

'Possibly a little clearer understanding of certain types of people,' said Adam, looking at her a bit hesitantly. 'I checked the classified pages of the telephone directory today to see if there was any sort of school I thought would help me, but I didn't find anything.'

'But it couldn't be too difficult if all you really need is an understanding of people,' Janet said. She was in her element, knowing that when she was actually involved in counselling she was on firm ground. 'I'm certain we could work that out.'

'Do you mean you'd work with me?' asked Adam, looking hopeful.

'Well, if there's no other way, I'm sure we could manage it,' Janet said. She should direct and encourage rather than actually train a person for a job, but Adam Richfield was not exactly an ordinary case. Helping to guide him over the rough spots in forming a new career would be a new experience. She could derive considerable benefit from it. It would certainly be pleasant to work hand in hand with a man of his charms—calibre, she corrected herself immediately.

'Then you'd be willing to help me? You wouldn't laugh at me?' An anxiety she had not expected filled his voice.

'Of course I would,' she insisted. 'After all, that's the duty of a counsellor.' She said nothing about stretching those duties in his case.

He gave a deep sigh. 'That makes me feel so much better,' he said. 'But you give me your word you'll help me?'

'You have my word,' Janet said, feeling the warmth of a mother smiling at an anxious child. 'Now are you going to tell me what the wonderful new occupation is going to be?'

He nodded, shifted slightly so that he was partially turned, able to keep an eye on the road and yet judge her reaction. She congratulated herself that the nervousness, the shyness, had fallen away.

'Professional escort.'

Professional escort? Janet mentally lurched. She cast a quick glance out of the car window to assure herself the bump hadn't been physical. At first she couldn't speak. Her mental tape recorder was playing back the memory of the last few minutes of conversation complete with video. His shyness, his hesitancy, his entire attitude had been a sham leading her on to give him encouragement and—and a commitment to *help* him!

Unable to both drive the car and keep a constant watch on Janet, he was trying to divide his attention equally between the two when a small sports car pulled into the traffic from the airport entrance. It sailed across two lanes of traffic, directly into his path. Adam gave his attention to his driving and handled in a masterly fashion what could have been a serious accident.

Janet watched him, sizzling inside because she knew she'd been set up. He'd planned his little scheme with the thoroughness he probably put into one of his robberies. And he wasn't getting away with it! She knew what he was expecting. He was relying on her mid-West farming country morality to cause her to throw up her hands, insist he was beyond hope, and demand to be returned home. But she had a little surprise in store for him. She might be a fresh-faced Iowa farm girl, but he'd learn that those Hawkeyes had a little more to them than he expected.

'I see,' she said slowly, as though her mind was truly on his proposed occupation. 'Do you propose to work for another company or would you be starting your own business?'

She was rewarded by a wary glance.

'Oh, I thought my own business,' he said. 'It shouldn't

take much in the way of overheads. I was thinking of brochures in the hotels, ads in the paper, and maybe the yellow pages.'

His mention of advertising brought Janet up short for a moment. Obviously he saw the surprised look in her eye, for his white teeth flashed in a grin.

'I said an escort service. I didn't say I was going to set up as a prostitute!'

'I didn't say you did,' Janet retorted, her face suffusing with colour. 'I—er—I——' Somehow the words wouldn't come.

'The object, Miss Talbot,' his tone was superior, 'was to find gainful employment in a lawful occupation. Not to start a secondary set of misdemeanours.'

'Most certainly,' Janet answered back. 'But I can't see that I'd be any help.'

'But you already have been,' he assured her. With a sweeping hand, he indicated the suit and the car. 'You've given me the courage to get this far. And I promise you, the suit is new. I'm sure if you inspect me closely, there's probably a tag still hanging on it somewhere.'

Janet knew that remark was pure fallacy. The suit might, indeed, be new, but she very much doubted if even a man of Adam Richfield's quick decision could get a completely tailored suit within forty-eight hours. Nor did she think they came with store tags! Never having been in a position to get her clothes custom-made, she wasn't quite sure of that last assumption. Apparently not realising she'd caught his small lie, he was continuing.

'I know San Diego. I have a weakness for good restaurants. I like atmosphere. I know the tourist places. I think I have the makings of a good escort—or guide,' he shrugged. His blue eyes twinkled with mishchief. 'And if I understood you correctly, even you

were willing to admit I might have certain, though
possibly slight, attributes that would make me agree-
able to female company.'

Janet felt her jaw tighten. Her muscles were
demanding a chance to chew up and and destroy her
words of two nights before.

CHAPTER FOUR

JANET was unsure whether her primary emotion was anger, suspicion, or a deep desire to demand to be returned to the Binns' house after Adam made his announcement. She really wanted to turn tail and run, she decided. He had truly understood her mid-Western thinking. Her list of serious occupations was made up of the normal jobs: doctors, lawyers, mechanics, barbers, accountants, truck drivers, and the out-of-the-ordinary computer people who parked their cars at odd angles and talked in an incomprehensible jargon. A professional escort service was totally out of her realm of thinking.

She turned her eyes to gaze at Adam Richfield, trying again to peer beneath the poised surface of his expression, wondering if he was joking or trying to shock her.

He was concentrating on his driving. They'd left the scenic bay front and he was preparing to make a left turn. The banks, fast-food restaurants, clothing stores and service stations could have lined any street in the country, and only the occasional palm tree or twisting juniper reminded her she was in California.

But the distance they travelled while still remaining within the metropolis was bewildering. Janet knew from having explored an area map that the city of San Diego was huge. Adding to the stranger's confusion were numerous other political boundaries, small cities whose borders intertwined with San Diego and each other until the metropolitan area held almost half as many people as the entire state of Iowa.

She wondered how long she would feel confused and lost, and thought maybe Adam Richfield had a better idea with his escort service than she had at first supposed. As a new resident, and one who planned to stay for some time, she could slowly learn her way around. But what about the person in town on business? Or the two-week vacationer? A professional escort, one who knew the town, the best places to dine, the most interesting scenery, could prevent a lot of disappointments, she thought.

That was, she amended, pulling her distrust to the front of her mind again, if Adam Richfield was not pulling her leg.

She still wasn't sure.

While he manoeuvred the car through traffic, she watched him. Her sense of being lost came from more than the physical disorientation of not knowing the city. She didn't understand this man and was bothered by her confusion. In someone else she might find the job of professional escort suitable. But he just didn't *fit*! She tried to marshal her thoughts, her impressions, anything that would reinforce that instinctive reaction. He gave the appearance of being able to handle almost anything. His hands, resting lightly on the steering wheel, were strong, long-fingered, his right middle finger slightly calloused, as though he held a pen or pencil for long hours.

Why would a professional burglar write so much? she wondered. She didn't want more questions. She wanted answers.

His strong profile was set in thoughtful lines, and while she watched him he seemed to reach some decision. His shoulders, already straight, drew back almost imperceptibly, but the slight raising of his chin indicated that he'd set some course and was determined to see it through.

Full speed ahead and damn the torpedoes, Janet thought as she watched him. He could be a ship's captain, on the board of directors of some conglomerate, the owner of his own company. He didn't fit in the occupation he had chosen. For a man like Adam Richfield to do no more with his life than become a professional escort was similar to forcing a two-hundred-pound woman into a size eight dress.

While Janet's thoughts had been travelling independently, she was only dimly aware that they had left the business section behind and had been travelling down the street lined on both sides with boats and supply stores. At the end of several blocks, they had come out on a seaside park area. The movement of sails in the bay brought her out of her reverie just as Adam Richfield pulled into a parking lot. He eased the car into a space with the expertise that fitted the new image. As he walked round to open the door for her, Janet came to a decision. He had no more intention of becoming a personal escort than she did of taking up volleyball for a living! He was using his choice of occupation to make her give up. He wasn't getting away with it. He'd find she could wait him out. When he opened the door and offered her his hand, she took it demurely.

'I assume women still like to be assisted from a car,' he said. 'Maybe you could tell me whether my future client's would appreciate it or find it chauvinistic.'

'Oh, I think they'd appreciate it,' said Janet, waiting for him to close the door and lock the car.

He took her arm as they crossed the parking lot, but while other couples seemed to be heading for the main entrance, the light pressure of his fingers guided her towards a wooden gate to the right of the restaurant. He led her into a small sheltered Oriental garden where a fountain and waterfall created out of giant clam shells fed a pool shaded by a large tree.

'I'm not sure we're supposed to enter this way, but it creates a more romantic setting, I think.'

'For who? And why?' Janet asked, her suspicions bared. But she couldn't resist stepping across the little curved bridge, though it led not to the restaurant, but to the other side of the pool.

'For my prospective clients,' Adam answered, as though she'd be foolish to think anything else.

Janet blushed, and was glad she was on the bridge where her footing required her attention. 'I thought you said you wouldn't be a gigolo,' she snapped, refusing to let him think she considered his romantic ideas included her.

'Then maybe I have the wrong idea entirely,' he said as he put one foot on the bridge, preparing to join her.

But Janet, already wary because of her own discomfort, stepped hastily off the other end, strolled over to an opening in the sheltering foliage and gazed out at the bay.

'I thought the general idea,' Adam went on, 'was to create an illusion that no one was to take seriously. Of course——'

While he was speaking he was coming nearer and Janet stood poised on the walkway, knowing there was nowhere to go unless she decided to take the precarious climb down to the rocks in the bay some six feet below.

'I can't see starting a successful escort service by taking the client into a restaurant and dumping her on a chair like a sack of groceries.'

While his last words held nothing romantic for Janet, he was standing so close behind her that his breath stirred her hair. And the shiver that ran up her spine had nothing to do with the cooling evening.

With a quick step to the side, she increased the distance between them and turned to gaze at the little decorative garden. 'I think you're forgetting there should be some practicalities along with your glamour,' she said. 'If you brought the hypothetical client here to dinner after a day of seeing the sights, her attention might be centred on her aching feet.' She waved her hand, indicating the garden. 'There's no place to sit.'

'Oomph!' Adam raised a protective hand, holding it across his stomach as though he'd been struck. 'A lesson learned.'

'Moreover,' Janet went on as she used the walk to stroll over to look down the path leading to the restaurant, 'I would say we've entered from the wrong direction and you should let the designers of the restaurant be your guide. Obviously they intended couples to walk out in this direction.' She looked round critically and nodded to the torch-topped poles that had not yet been lit since dusk was still an hour away. 'Torchlight and moonlight would make it far more effective.'

'And the client's feet would have had time to rest during dinner,' Adam said with a half-smile. 'You underestimate your talents in training, Miss Talbot.' With a few quick steps he crossed the bridge Janet had skirted in her attempt to put some distance between them, and joined her on the path.

His hand lay gently, almost casually on her back as he guided her in the direction of the restaurant. His touch created a focus of warmth in her, threatening to pull her attention away from everything but the man walking by her side. She warned herself again to remember that he was just a client. The last thing she needed was another Derek in her life. And he could certainly be successful if he were serious about this new career. The quiet elegance of his clothing, the casual assurance with which he approached the restuarant, showed no desire to draw attention to himself. Nor could it hide the sensual air of masculinity that hung about him like an aura, drawing the eyes of the people they passed. Janet felt as if she was enveloped in some cocoon of reflected glow, as though just being at his side enhanced her own femininity.

His female clients would vie for that atmosphere, she thought. Yes, he could be successful. She tried to imagine another women walking the same path with him. She wondered why she couldn't feel the same enthusiasm she had seen in Bob's face when his client, Sarah, had come in with news of her success in starting a new life.

The idea of another woman walking beside Adam Richfield caused Janet to feel lonely. Her feeling wasn't helped when three stylish young women rounded the path. They were grouped together as they made some comment on their evening, their eyes bright, happy, and expectant. As they caught sight of Adam and Janet, their gazes lingered on him and quickened with interest. They exchanged speaking looks before forming a single file to pass.

'Prospective clients,' Janet said as the girls passed by and resumed their conversation once they were out of hearing. 'Or old friends?' she asked.

Adam shrugged, his face carefully impassive. 'Don't know them. Maybe they belong to a rival gang,' he said, adroitly turning the conversation into other channels.

'I don't doubt it.' Janet strolled on as he stepped up beside her again when the path was clear. 'You brought me to the local hangout——' With a negligent wave of her hand, she indicated the small pier and the private docks off the to right where several boats were resting easily on the calm water. 'And I suppose those boats have brought in the big crime bosses from New York, Italy, Florida and——'

'Peru,' he finished when she'd run out of locations. 'We do a big business in smuggled llamas.'

Janet smiled at his sally and strolled along. Her attitude of severity had dropped away. Fleetingly she thought she shouldn't be joking with him about crime. But the semi-tropical atmosphere, the South Seas décor, enhanced by the torches that were now being lit, and the laughter of people enjoying the restaurant pushed away the memories of two nights before when she'd awakened to hear a 'thump' and had turned on the lights to find a burglar in the hallway.

She tried to remind herself that the burglar was now standing by her side. Associating him with those memories was becoming more difficult.

The path curved round the lower level of the restaurant. They looked in on diners who had an unrestricted view of the harbour with only occasional interruptions by the strollers on the path. For patrons who desired to enjoy the soft cool evening, a few steps away another wooden gate and hedge partially screened a large patio for outdoor dining. It gave a totally unobstructed view of the bay and the San Diego skyline.

'Seems as though my Cook's tour of inspection did bring us in the wrong way,' said Adam, looking round while the waiters hurried back and forth. They saw no sign of a host or hostess in that part of the restaurant.

Janet, admiring the South Sea totem poles, turned to ask if they should retrace their steps and go in the proper entrance. She was just in time to see Adam's gaze fall upon a diner on the patio. Adam tensed and turned away quickly, but not fast enough for the gentleman raising his eyes from his plate to miss catching sight of them. Though he was too far away for Janet to see his eyes, the suddenly arrested movement of his head told her that he recognised her escort.

'You know, ravioli's just the thing.' Adam caught her arm. He swung her round so quickly that she staggered, and hustled her up the path in the direction they had come. Janet made no demur at their speed. She could feel his urgent need to get away. But once outside the wooden gates, she pulled her arm from his grasp and gazed up at him. All the old suspicions were back. He was once again the housebreaker she'd caught two nights before.

'Was he a cop?' she demanded. She interpreted the startled look he threw her as surprise that she could put two and two together so easily. 'I'm not stupid,' she reminded him. 'And you should be aware that as long as you remain in San Diego, occasionally your past will find you when you least expect it.'

'Apparently,' he said as they headed for the car.

As he manoeuvred the car out of the parking lot, Janet sat back and considered the aborted trip to Bali Hai and the man driving the car. Her emotions were whirling like the spinning of the steering wheel as it straightened after the sharp turn on to the street.

Adam Richfield wasn't the only one who had suffered a shock, though for an entirely different reason. Even though she'd given lip service to his rehabilitation, she'd been slowly forgetting the purpose of the evening. The atmosphere, the torches, the laughter of the other diners, and the physical attraction of the man by her side had been sneaking round her counsellor detachment. She felt like a sunbather warmed through by the sun and suddenly slapped by a cold wave of reality. The memories of the past few minutes pointed an accusing finger. She'd even been envious of his prospective clients! She shifted uncomfortably, as if part of her mind was putting the other half in a spotlight, baring all her indiscretions for public viewing. She made herself a promise not to make another slip.

Physically reacting to her decision, she straightened, placed her feet together and folded her hands over her handbag. Her voice was as prim as her posture. 'It's just as well the incident occurred. We always pay for our past sins in some way.'

The quirk of his lips quickly straightened, threw her off stride, but she struggled to pick up the thread of the point she intended to make. 'You've choosen a highly visible career and you must expect to run into your past from time to time.'

'I suppose I could relocate. Go to another city and begin again,' Adam agreed.

Janet's mind was immediately full of objections, a muddle of irrational 'but's and 'don't's with no clear reasoning behind them. She strove for logic to counter his suggestion and grasped at the first straw. 'Do you know any other city well enough to be successful?' she asked.

He shook his head. 'Not really.'

'I think you said you'd never been arrested.'

'No, I've never been arrested,' he agreed.

'Then do many cops know you by sight?'

That quirk was back on his lips again. 'No, I can honestly say not many would.'

Janet allowed some time to pass while she thought that over. 'Well, you shouldn't be harassed. I think you should brave it out. If you had an actual client with you, you simply couldn't bolt out of a restaurant and take her into some hole-in-the-wall.'

'No, I don't suppose I could,' he said. His left hand lying on the steering wheel shifted. He flipped the blinker and made a U-turn.

'Are we going back to the Bali Hai?'

'No, but I promise you it won't be a hole-in-the-wall,' he said.

Janet was pleased at his reversal. 'And no matter who's in the restaurant, we're going to continue?' she asked.

'Let's say we're going to start out with that plan in mind,' Adam answered. He still seemed wary, but at least he wasn't running.

She relaxed and gave him a smile. 'You just pretend I'm a client and let's see how the rest of the evening goes.'

He divided his time between watching the street and the buildings they passed, but took a moment to raise an eyebrow. 'Does that mean you're going to pick up the bill?'

'Forget it. Consider it charge for the course.'

Adam Richfield was as good as his word. One would think, as the hostess led them through the dining-room of Humphrey's and out on to the patio, that his past had been so exemplary it would never occur to him to fear some memory out of the shadows. He learned his lessons well, Janet thought with a combination of pride and an emptiness. Her feelings were born out of the knowledge that all the attributes necessary for him to begin his new career were already developed in Adam Richfield. And he would soon be moving forward in his career with no need for her guidance or help.

'It seems we'll still have a view of the bay,' he said as they were seated on the patio overlooking a yacht basin. A glass wall protected them from the evening breeze. Above their heads stars twinkled around the scalloped edges of the table umbrellas. The yacht basin was crowded. Boats with shrouded sails rocked gently in the wake of the incoming craft. Across the bay, the ridge of Point Loma was decorated with the lights of the houses on the hill. Out on the bay the triangular sails of boats yet to make harbour semed to drift disembodied in the twilight.

For a moment, Janet was so caught up with the scene that she felt a little resentment when her view was disturbed by the waitress, who brought a breadboard on which a round loaf of wheat bread shared space with a dish of whipped butter. She turned her attention back to the table and became aware of Adam Richfield's perusal. She blushed slightly when she realised she had allowed the view to totally distract her. 'Toto, something tells me we're not in Iowa any more,' she said, paraphrasing the famous Dorothy.

Adam had opened his menu while the waitress stood waiting. He glanced down at it and then back at Janet with amusement in his eyes. 'Oh, but we're well supplied with all the ordinary items. Would you care for a cup of cocoa?'

Of all the things he could have suggested, nothing could have surprised Janet more, and she opened the menu to see what he meant.

Among the drinks that were listed as 'Specialties of the House' was indeed cocoa, called on the menu 'Killer Cocoa', made of Rumple Minzt and hot chocolate.

'Sounds deliciously dangerous, and I think I'll leave it alone,' Janet said, her eyes continuing down the list.

The next drink to catch her eyes had a rather long name, 'Get Potted at Humphrey's', followed by '(You keep the Pot)'. According to the menu, it contained three rums blended with fruit juices and served in a monogrammed glass flowerpot. The drink was large enough for two. Trying to envisage it, Janet raised her eyes thoughtfully and met Adam's across the table. The memory of her inebriation two evenings before caused her to blush slightly, and she hurriedly decided on a *cappuccino* while he ordered a Scotch and water.

When the waitress moved away from the table, Janet allowed her gaze to travel back to the bay again, though her attention was clearly fixed on the man across the table. The swings in his attitude were confusing her. If his shyness and uncertanties on the drive to the Bali Hai had been real, he was certainly covering them well. She couldn't prevent a lingering suspicion that his announced intention of becoming a professional escort was a ruse, but she was determined to play the game.

Yet there was certainly nothing phoney about his desire not to meet the man at the Bali Hai. Then she wondered why that hesitation should have surprised her. Looking back, she realised he'd only reinforced what she already knew.

But at that point he interrupted her thinking. 'I'm curious,' he said, drawing her gaze back to the table. 'You can give me a woman's opinion. As a stranger in town, do you prefer looking at the view uninterrupted, or should I be making some conversation?'

Janet couldn't help but admire him. If he was just pretending to be interested in being a professional escort, he certainly played the part well. She waited until the waitress, who was just approaching the table, had left their drinks and steaming bowls of creamy fish chowder and moved away. Then she answered.

'I think that depends upon the woman,' she said thoughtfully. 'Some like to chatter, some don't. Personally, I like to savour experiences. Like this chowder.'

'You're saying some women are savourers,' he murmured, raising a spoonful of the mixture from his bowl. His eyes twinkled with some joke Janet wasn't sure she caught.

Dividing her attention between the chowder and the man across the table, she decided to let the last remark pass. She wasn't sure she liked that gleam in his eye. What was he planning now? she wondered. She recognised an undercurrent of double meaning in what he'd said and came mentally to attention, then relaxed, deciding his verbal ploy didn't refer to her personally.

'You'll have to judge each of your clients individually,' she warned him. 'One will be looking for a mild flirtation, the next may want an impersonal guide.'

'I thought all women wanted the illusion of romance,' Adam said.

Janet looked out at the lights of the houses on the ridge of the Point Loma peninsula. Down in the bay, a boat was moving slowly to its berth. Its wake caused the docked boats to rock gently, their tall masts swaying, so that the lights on the hill appeared to blink with a holiday spirit.

Across the candlelit table, Adam was watching her. The flickering light brought out the strong planes of his rugged face. Against the background of a piano somewhere in the building, the hum of conversation from the other tables created a cosy atmosphere. His eyes, reflecting the candlelight, seemed to promise all the thrills dreamed of in the romantic heart but seldom found in reality. Hold it! Janet strongly curbed her imagination, reminding herself why she was there. Time to bring back order and purpose to the conversation.

'Women want *romance*,' she warned him. 'Many don't know the difference between illusion and the real thing.'

'You're saying I'd better be careful?'

'You could end up with an exclusive contract. And that smile says you're not taking me seriously.'

'Oh, I am,' Adam answered meekly.

She didn't for a moment believe the sudden innocence of his expression. She was poised to give him a lecture when the waitress came to remove the empty soup bowls and place their dinner before them. But by the time she moved away again, Adam's mind had apparently turned in another direction.

'I'm curious,' he said as he picked up the napkin-wrapped lemon and squeezed it, allowing the juice to flavour the king crab. 'What caused you to choose your occupation?'

With the tines of her fork, Janet idly destroyed the perfect edging of the flaky golden pastry dish of salmon as she thought about his question. She'd always known the answer, but how did you express it to a person like Adam Richfield?

'Because of my father,' she said. 'He was in the police force until he was permanently disabled in a shoot-out with a robber.'

Adam looked a little surprised. 'I'd think that would leave bitterness, not a desire to help.'

'Maybe, if my father had dwelled on a lot of yesterdays, but he's always a tomorrow man,' Janet acknowledged. 'But he's too fine a man for bitterness. He believes rehabilitation might have prevented his tragedy and that of many others.'

'Admirable,' Adam nodded, but he went no further with the conversation.

From the piano bar came the first notes of *My Wild Irish Rose*, which were lost under a chorus of voices joining in. And behind Adam and Janet three tables of tourists who were sitting over their drinks also joined in the song.

As they finished their dinner, one song seemed to drift into another. The unseen pianist was in a mellow mood, and the blending of voices carried out across the patio, melting into the soft night. Twilight drifted into darkness, the candles on the tables reflecting against the glass windscreen, and as Janet gazed at it she noticed one particular couple reflected against the darkness. The blonde woman who raised her head was being watched by the striking dark-haired man at the table. Janet caught her breath as she took in his soft, gentle expression, and a feeling of loneliness filled her. Though she was the blonde who sat in that chair, his look was meant for another time, another place, a night that could lead to the development of more than just a client/counsellor relationship.

She was both relieved and sad when they left the restaurant. But apparently the evening wasn't over. When they left the parking lot, Adam drove at a leisurely pace down the island, following the pavement as it circled the Friendship Bell and returned. Along the shore a grass lawn spread to the rock-lined embankment that prevented the restless waters from eroding the island. The gentle breeze of the evening barely disturbed the water, and from across the bay the reflection seemed to magnify the city.

'It's really beautiful,' Janet murmured.

'Something for everyone in San Diego,' Adam answered. 'For sand fanatics we have the beaches. For those who like their waterfronts civilised——' He pulled the car into a parking area and brought it to a stop. That unreal postcard feeling was back again as he got out of the car and came round to open her door.

They strolled along the concrete walk, a clearly defined white ribbon against the grass on either side. To the right the bank twenty feet away dropped down to the water, where the whisper of waves made a soft background song for the view.

Across the bay the silhouette of San Diego, many of its buildings indistinct in the darkness, seemed to consist of columns of lights reaching up into the dark sky. Their reflections on the dark water wavered slightly, like beckoning fingers stretching out over the water.

'Beautiful,' murmured Janet, caught up in the view. She let her gaze travel from the reflection, back to the lights of the city where they mingled with the stars of the clear night. Slightly to her left and above her head, an ornamental date palm stretched the silhouette of its long fronds into the soft night.

Lowering her gaze slightly, she realised that Adam

was watching her with a strange intensity. A street light some distance away illuminated only part of his face and shadowed his eyes. The small quirk of amusement that had been so prevalent during the evening had disappeared entirely.

She was aware of his hand on her arm, of his closeness, of the measure of warmth that seemd to be protecting her from the breeze coming in off the ocean. He stepped closer, a fluid movement hardly recognisable. But with his increased nearness, the view seemed to drop away in her renewed awareness of him. With a strange slowness, a deliberateness of movement, he pulled the folded shawl from where it hung over her arm and let it fall open, sliding it though his fingers until he held it almost centred, the tasselled end of the triangular lace falling in soft folds. His eyes, still shadowd, were pools of unreadable shadows as he stepped closer. With his left hand he brought the soft fabric round behind her. The lace brushed her arm, a whisper of a touch that ran through her nerves in a thrill of expectancy.

Reaching behind her with his other hand, he caught up the soft fabric and slowly draped it round her shoulders. His hands were occupied with the shawl, but in draping it against her back and across her shoulders his fingers lightly touched her, and seemed to burn a brand of sensation that encircled and trapped her.

With agonising slowness, he drew the silky lace across her arm, allowing the tassels to tease her skin, skin already tortured by the emotion raised by those shadowed eyes.

With an equal slowness, he brought the other end round and draped it across her left shoulder, bringing his arm round again to straighten a fold behind her neck. His eyes, holding her with their shadowed intensity all the greater for not being fully seen, held her hypnotically as his fingers travelled from the shawl to caress the back of her neck. His other arm encircled her as his lips came down to meet hers.

Caught up in his arms, Janet felt a burst of dammed-up emotion. Some hidden resource within herself had exploded and filled her with an indescribable hunger for an unrealised and dimly viewed ecstacy. Desire rushed through her, flooding her senses. She yielded to the tightening of his arms, allowing him to mould her body to fit the contours of his own. Over the rhythm of her rapidly beating heart, she could feel his. She was pressed against him, almost bruised with the pressure of his chest, his strong tight thighs. Her breath seemed entirely gone, but swept up in the kiss, she felt no need of it.

His release caught her unaware and she nearly stumbled as he stepped back. All her senses were screaming, as if they had been robbed of some vital life-giving force. She gasped, drawing in the breath the sudden kiss had robbed her of, and she stared at him, shaken and confused.

Adam also took a deep breath, and his innocent expression helped to rob her of breath again when he spoke.

'Should that be part of the service? Or should I charge extra?'

CHAPTER FIVE

AT six-thirty the next morning Adam Richfield carried his second cup of coffee into his office and pushed a few papers around on his desk as he tried to find a coaster on which to set the cup. Tiring of the search, he flipped over a legal pad. He used the cardboard back to soak up whatever circles the cup might leave. He turned his executive chair slightly sideways and raised his feet, crossing them on the corner of the desk. Another legal pad and a pencil lay in easy reach as he sat waiting.

Within a couple of minutes he expected Rhoda to come bouncing in with an energy indecent at six-thirty in the morning. But he couldn't complain about it. The actual workday for the office didn't begin until eight. In the summer the surveyors began their day earlier than the rest of the company, and Adam was always in for a last-minute check with his party chiefs.

Rhoda came in early to give any instructions on additional information needed by her department. That particular morning, Norman had also been early with some questions from the architects.

As Adam expected, Rhoda soon appeared at the doorway, walking a little more slowly and more carefully than usual. Her own coffee cup appeared to be over-full and she was giving all her attention to it. In her other hand she carried the battered shorthand pad on which she took her daily notes.

Early morning was a good time for their conferences. They were uninterrupted by telephone calls and other distractions. They could discuss the jobs in progress, estimates for those they hoped to get and problems with the employees without worrying about being overheard.

But Rhoda, well aware of Adam's activity the night before, wasn't interested in business.

'How did it go?' she asked, her eyes lively.

'None of your business.'

'Sure it is. I was in on the beginning.'

Adam knew she wouldn't leave him alone until he answered her. She might even help him straighten out his mental tangle.

'It was the damnedest mess I've ever seen!'

'Well, did you get out of it? What happened?'

Adam gritted his teeth, but he couldn't prevent the smile that kept creeping into his cheeks. He could feel his eyes narrow with it. He was slightly angry with himself, with Janet Talbot, and yet the ridiculousness of the situation made him want to laugh.

'I've really put my foot in it now,' he said with a slight shake of his head.

'Well, what did you do?'

As he kept staring at her, trying to figure out exactly how to put it in words, Rhoda bounced on the chair in anticipation. If she gained another twenty pounds, he'd have to get that chair reinforced.

'Are you going to tell me or not?' she demanded. 'If you don't, I warn you I won't do a thing all day.'

Adam grinned as he told the story on himself. 'I figured out the perfect way to get that broad off my back. I picked an occupation—remember I *told* you I had to pick an occupation?'

'Yeah, go on—go on.'

'I picked an occupation guaranteed to chase her all the way back to Iowa.'

'What was it?'

'Professional escort.'

Those two words were an emotional bomb. Rhoda exploded with laughter. 'Boss, you're vicious,' she said, laughing again.

'Not vicious enough,' Adam said. 'She bought it. Hook, line and sinker.'

Rhoda stopped laughing and stared at him in surprise. 'She believed you?'

'She not only *believed* me, she's going to help me with my training.'

'Good God!' Rhoda muttered breathlessly, staring into the distance of her own vision. 'She's pulling your leg.'

'No, I pulled her leg and got away with it. Which got me trapped,' Adam argued. 'Now I don't know what to do.'

'Well—well, how did the evening go?' asked Rhoda.

'Pretty damned uncomfortable. Particularly when we went in the Bali Hai. The first person I saw was Fred Mosley.'

'*Our* Fred Mosley of Cedar Heights?'

'Right. And he'd have blown my act if I'd given him a chance. He'd have walked right up to the table and argued about why we can't totally fill that little canyon.'

'He would have,' Rhoda agreed, 'and blown everything. Wait a minute. If he had, she would have known the truth.'

'And might have created a scene,' Adam argued.

He wasn't sure Janet would have caused any embarrassment, as a matter of fact he doubted it. But he wasn't ready to examine those thoughts too closely. Conversation with Mosley would have brought questions from Janet Talbot that would have freed him from the situation, but he didn't want to think about that either.

His memories kept returning to her sparkling eyes as she admired the view. That little-girl expectancy while he had sliced the loaf of wheat bread at Humphrey's, her delight over a salmon puff pastry, and a childlike curiosity over the decoration on a chocolate mousse pie.

'It's a chocolate *nut*,' she'd said in wonder as she chewed thoughtfully. He had a mental picture of her as a little girl, eating the candy candle-holders off her birthday cake.

But intruding into all those memories were her eyes when they'd stood on the walk and he'd put the shawl round her shoulders. Her eyes had been wide with wonder and an expectancy filled with hesitation, as if she hadn't understood her own feelings.

Nor, he had to admit, had he understood his.

He'd pulled a purely jackass stunt with the remark he'd made when he let her go. Strictly a matter of self-defence, he told himself. He was a fool to have left the Bali Hai. If he hadn't, she'd know the truth and he'd be out of his situation.

'Well, what are you going to do?' asked Rhoda. 'How long are you going to play this silly game?' Suddenly her eyes turned shrewd. 'Or are you going to play it as long as you can?'

'Cut that out!' Adam ordered. Suddenly all the humour was gone. Rhoda Manion was his best friend, but he wasn't allowing her or anyone else to question his sudden indecision that was creating more problems than he could handle.

But Rhoda hadn't taken offence at his sharpness. She never did. He often suspected her of goading him and taking it as a triumph when she drove him to lose his temper.

'Just remember Mama Confessor is here if you need her,' she said, grinning, and flipped open her shorthand pad, putting an end to the personal side of the conversation. 'If Billy doesn't hit any snags,' she said, consulting her notes, 'he should finish the contours on Cedar Heights today——'

She paused as the door to the office echoed a tap and

opened. Norman came into the room.

'I've got a problem,' he said.

'Join the crowd,' Rhoda answered him. Her grin, for Adam only, referred back to their conversation.

But Norman hadn't seen it and didn't catch the humour. 'I hate to jump to the front of the line,' he said, 'but we don't have either the preliminary specs or the computations on the Wainwright job.'

Adam, who had picked up his pencil to make notes on what Rhoda had been ready to say, laid it down again. 'You mean they were left at Harry's when we got the plans? What's the problem? Run out another copy on the computer—oh, *damn* Harry!'

Norman, meeting Adam's eyes squarely, nodded. 'You know Harry.'

Adam was occasionally irritated by his junior partner's distrust of computers, but until now the quirk hadn't caused any severe difficulties. Harry worked out his computations on the small programmable calculator and kept them in longhand. There was only one copy. When he checked the job he would have used them, so they were probably still at his house.

'You checked his desk in the drafting room?'

Norman nodded to Adam's question.

'How about in his office?' Adam was clutching at straws.

'Not there. They must be at the house, Boss.'

'We'll have to get 'em. Wainwright goes over every figure—not that he knows what he's seeing——'

'But they have to be here,' Norman agreed.

'I still have my dark clothes,' said Rhoda. 'Here's what we can do. You take Janet Talbot out to dinner and Norman and I will get in the house——'

'Yeah, I know how to get in the window,' Norman said hesitantly. 'The only problem is—has she had that burglar alarm connected?'

'*I* don't know. She didn't say anything about it,' said Adam, idly scribbling on the pad, and looked down to realise he was drawing a window with bars on it, which brought him up short. He turned to glare at the two project managers as if the turn of the conversation was their fault.

'What's all this burglary stuff again?' he demanded. 'We broke into the house the first time because we didn't know we had a choice. Call Janet Talbot and ask for them.'

The other two looked at him as if he'd lost his mind.

'You mean just *call*?' Rhoda frowned. 'Somehow that seems a little flat.'

'You're not going to be satisfied until you get me in jail,' said Adam, pointing a pencil at her.

'Well, we *could* call, I guess.' Norman, for all his calm and usually serious exterior, also looked a little disappointed.

'I'm going to inventory the pencils!' Adam warned. 'You two have a streak of dishonesty. Now back to Janet. She wouldn't know Norman or his voice.' He looked up at the architectural project manager. 'You call, tell her where you think they might be. She shouldn't have any trouble finding them. She's a bright girl—in some ways. Then run over and pick them up.' His gaze switched from Norman to Rhoda, who showed her understanding with a sly smile.

When Norman had left the room, Adam and Rhoda went back to the discussion of the daily schedule. Adam was involved in working up an estimate for a conservation dam when Norman stuck his head in the door an hour later.

'I called her,' he said. 'She wasn't sure if she'd have time to find them this morning, but she'd be sure to locate them this afternoon.'

Two hours later, not entirely satisfied with his

estimate, Adam shoved a sheaf of assembled papers into a manila file folder, labelled it with the job name, and closed it with a finality born of frustration. He hadn't been able to keep his mind on his work. Janet Talbot kept intruding into his thoughts.

Restless, he left his office, strolled down the hall, and looked in the various offices. At the back of the building he entered the empty survey rooms, picked up some scattered notebooks on the large drafting table, idly thumbed through them and stacked them in a neat pile. Then he started back up the hallway to his office.

He saw Rhoda as she passed Jenny's desk with a nod and entered the open door of his office. She'd just moved out of sight when the hiss of the front door alerted him that someone had entered the building. He saw the slim feminine figure with familiar dark blonde hair. Her back was to the hallway as she stood in front of Jenny's desk. Her voice was low, but it carried to Adam as she asked to see a Mr Norman Edwards. Rhoda, just coming out of Adam's office, stiffened as she heard the name, and apparently recognised the manila folder Janet was carrying.

Knowing he could be caught in the hall and faced with having to make an explanation in the hearing of his employees, Adam ducked into the shallow space between an alcove and the large blueprinting machine. He stooped down. Rhoda, hurrying down the hall, saw him slip out of sight and also ducked in behind the machine.

'Get out of here!' he whispered urgently, glaring at Rhoda for being stupid enough to emulate him.

'I can't let her *see* me,' Rhoda insisted, her voice half-panicked.

'Why not?' Adam whispered back, disgusted. 'She doesn't know you from Adam.'

'Eve,' Rhoda corrected him. 'I don't *know* why—but

I'm not moving.'

While they'd been arguing, Jenny had called Norman over the intercom. Through the open door they heard the conversation, the garbled sound of voices echoing themselves when the ear could pick up both the original remark and the fractional delay caused by the electronic mechanism.

Norman came up the hall and stopped when he saw Rhoda and Adam behind the print machine. 'What's up?' he asked, looking down at them.

'We're fixing the machine,' Rhoda told him. 'Get out of here. Get up to the front desk.'

'But——' Norman started to object.

Adam waved him away, pointing urgently towards the front of the building. All they needed was for Janet to turn, see Norman, and decide to meet him halfway down the hall. Norman looked in the direction Adam was pointing to and his face paled. He swallowed convulsively and continued on up the hall.

'He looked guilty as sin,' Rhoda whispered to Adam. 'She'll have to know something's going on.' Then her head jerked back in his direction. 'She'll see your name on the door.'

'Did you close it?' asked Adam.

Rhoda was thoughtful, then she brightened. 'No.'

Still squatting behind the print machine, they listened to the conversation at the desk.

'I found these this morning,' Janet was saying. 'I hope they're what you're looking for.'

'Er—er—yes,' Norman was stammering. They heard the soft sound as he flipped through the forms. 'They all seem to be here. We could have picked them up.' He sounded to Adam as if he had a frog in his throat.

'Maybe I was silly,' Janet confessed, 'but I felt as if I should bring them myself. I mean, since I'm staying in Mr Binns' house, I felt I should make sure I got them in the right hands.'

'Oh—er—I understand. Thanks a lot. I hope we won't have to bother you again ...' Norman was chattering, though the words cut off almost in mid-sentence with the closing of the front door.

'Get up!' Adam muttered to Rhoda, and they were both standing when Norman hurried back down the hall.

'I didn't tell her to bring them,' he insisted. 'I didn't have any idea——'

Just then Charlie, one of the new architectural draughtsmen, appeared round the corner, a large plan sheet in his hand. He was startled to find the senior partner of the company and the engineering project manager crammed in behind the print machine.

'And hereafter we'll be a little more careful of the prints we make,' Adam said loudly, realising he was covering one stupidity with another. At the moment *any*thing was preferable to giving an explanation to the architectural draughtsman.

Rhoda eased out from behind the machine and Adam followed her, starting up the hall. Then it occurred to him that he'd like to look over the information Janet had brought to assure himself she'd got all the papers. As he passed by the print alcove again, he saw the architectural draughtsman leaning across the machine, looking at the back of it. Further down the hall he found Rhoda leaning against the frame as though she'd been waiting for him.

'What's up?' he asked her.

'I was just thinking,' she said slowly, 'that's the second time in two days you've missed the chance to let Janet Talbot know the truth. I wonder why.'

'Go sweep the roof!' snapped Adam, and turned on his heel and strode back up the hall.

'Did it this morning!' she shouted after him.

When he entered his office, he slammed the door hard enough to knock off the nameplate had it not been firmly secured. Halfway to his desk, he stopped and looked at his watch. He'd give Janet Talbot exactly half an hour to return to her office, then he was going to pick up the phone, call her and tell her the truth.

If she didn't believe him, she could come back to the office and see. He had a business to run. He wasn't getting himself tied up with that broad. He was too busy for games, and it was time he told her.

Janet Talbot wasn't returning to the office. Her visit to Associated Architects and Engineers had been unplanned, or at least unplanned for that morning.

As part of her job she was familiarising herself with the local opportunities for the clients of Venitia House, and the state unemployment office was situated just over a block from Harry Binns' company. She had spotted it while she was looking for a parking place, and had decided to drop off the file before going on to her appointment.

Had Adam known it, he was the last person in the world she'd wanted to see that morning—or ever again, she told herself. She wasn't angry with him, though she'd been highly incensed at the remark he'd made after he'd kissed her by the bay. She was still shaken and more concerned with her own emotions.

If she allowed herself to do so, she could fall in love with Adam Richfield. She had faced that vulnerability, and it scared her. She wasn't in love with him right then, she decided, forcing that stricture on her feelings as if she was cramming a fat pair of hips into a girdle. She couldn't allow him to break her heart. She must learn to protect herself and her emotions. She was still too new at her occupation to be immune to the charms of endearing lawbreakers like Adam Richfield. Viewing him honestly, she wondered if she would ever be protected by someone with his magnetism. But self-preservation had come to the forefront of her mind. She'd been wrong to see him outside the atmosphere of the establishment in which she worked.

That had been her first error. Her second was frankly not recognising the dangers of becoming involved with a man of his charm.

The determination with which she held to her purpose was firm. It was as strong as the weight of her unhappiness was heavy. Her day was full of meetings. She lunched with a social worker and tried to assume an interest in a new federal training programme that was just being instigated in San Diego. On her way back to the office that afternoon she was filled with guilt over her thoughts of Adam, and wondered if she would remember a word about the new programme.

Back at her desk, she kept looking from her notes to the telephone. She jumped each time it rang, conscious of the disappointment as she took messages for other counsellors and for various members of the house.

Not until the bell sounded for the sixth time did her heart thrill to Adam Richfield's crisp masculine voice. But she'd made her decision. With a hoarseness born of self-inflicted pain, she identified herself when he asked for her by name.

'I'm sorry,' she said, before he could give her any answer. 'You've caught me at a bad time. I'll have to make this short.'

The silence at the other end of the phone seemed to drag out. 'I need to talk to you,' he said. He seemed to be put a bit off stride by her attitude.

'And I wanted to speak to you,' Janet answered quickly. She was weakening, she knew. She couldn't let the conversation drag out. 'I was very pleased with your progress last night. I feel you'll be able to go on with your ideas without any additional help from me.'

Silence again.

Say 'That's just fine' and hang up, Janet prayed, her heart fighting every word, but why prolong the inevitable?

'Thank you for your confidence,' he said, his voice ending on a note that made it seem as though he wanted to continue, but wasn't quite sure what to say.

'Good luck, and I'm sure you'll do very well,' Janet said. 'Oh, there's the other phone,' she lied, unable to continue the conversation further and not knowing how to say goodbye.

When she'd hung up she sat glowering at the telephone. Miserable instrument! she thought, resenting its unfeeling efficiency.

'He's out of my life,' she told herself. 'This is a big city. I don't have to see him again. I can forget him. What's an hour's conversation one night and dinner two nights later?'

She tried to visualise all the days in a lifetime. Those two interruptions in her life couldn't mean anything. By next week she wouldn't even remember him, she thought. She would. Once she developed new friends and a social life, she wouldn't even remember his name. She would.

A month from now, after she'd found her apartment, moved in, she'd be busy with her decorating. She'd be busy with her job. He'd be some vague memory of her first couple of days in San Diego. He'd blend in with a lot of experiences half-remembered. He wouldn't. No matter what she did, he'd stand out in her memory with a sharp-edged clarity of something one's dreamed of and lost.

Not lost, but thrown away, she told herself, and tried to pull herself back in focus. Adam Richfield was out of her life. The decision had been hers. There was no point in lying to herself, pretending she didn't care or that he had not existed. The memory of him wasn't like an old newspaper that could be thrown in the dustbin. She'd live with it for a while and she'd have to accept it.

Adam leaned back in his chair, put both hands on the yellow pencil and deliberately snapped it in half. He stared at it with irritation for a moment and then threw the two pieces down on the desk. After drumming his fingers on the chair arm and deriving no satisfaction from it, he pulled out the shallow desk drawer, and picked up another new yellow pencil. The virgin point put on it by Jenny was still sharp. He stared at it for the moment, and as deliberately as he had snapped the first one he broke the second. The door opened and Rhoda walked into his office.

She eyed the two broken pencils and looked up with no sign of humour in her eyes. 'Okay, which is it, the roof or the back alley?'

'Oh, shut up. Sit down. And close the door,' Adam growled.

'Which first?' she retorted as she shut the door behind her. She seemed to be taking an unholy satisfaction in his bad temper, as if she knew he'd been set down, and that didn't make him any happier.

She moved forward, took the chair, waited a moment and then gave a sigh. 'Okay, are we losing the company? Or is it something more serious?'

'I'm no longer being rehabilitated,' Adam said, his irritation flaring up suddenly. 'That damn broad just *dumped* me!'

Rhoda watched him for a moment and then smiled, her expression reminiscent. 'Welcome back to being fifteen. You didn't tell her the truth because you didn't want her to know.'

Adam glowered at her. 'You're trying to work this

into a romance.'

'No,' Rhoda said calmly, 'but I'm not blind.'

'If you don't have anything else to say, it's the back alley,' Adam retorted.

And after giving him a smile, Rhoda rose from the chair. 'I did come in for something—now I don't remember what.' At the door she turned back. 'You'd better get your love life straightened out, or none of us will get anything done.'

He opened his mouth to give her a scathing answer, but she jerked the door open, effectively silencing him. With a bright look, showing she knew exactly what she was doing, she pranced out and closed it behind her, leaving Adam with the additional frustration of not being able to retort.

If she wasn't careful, he'd fix her too. She was a good project manager and a good friend, and sometimes he forgot she was a woman—a woman with a lot of romantic ideas, trying to convince him his problems with Janet Talbot began and ended with love. She was out of her mind. Janet Talbot was an insufferable do-gooder, a know-it-all, and a silly little girl with her head on *sideways*. He was well out of it, and if he never saw her again he'd be lucky.

He reached in the drawer for another pencil while he repeated his litany of freedom, his fingers tightening on the slender wood and lead instrument until he'd snapped a third one. With an irritated sweep of his hand, he gathered up the pieces and dropped them in the waste paper basket. He reached into the console behind him and pulled out a new manila file folder. He labelled it with the name of a small job that would be his next estimating project. From the drawer he pulled out a pad of thin reproducible computation paper and repeated the name in the small block at the bottom.

Then, with both elbows leaning on the desk, he

remembered a bottle of champagne that had been cooling in his refrigerator for several weeks. If he drove over to Harry Binns' house that night . . . or perhaps he should wait a day . . . tomorrow was Friday . . .

When Janet left the office on Friday afternoon, she bought a newspaper and took it into a fast-food restaurant. She ate a hamburger without tasting it and made a careful list of apartments for rent. She drove by several, called on some others, and looked at four. They could not be as dreary as her depression made them appear, she thought. All but one had seemed in excellent repair, clean, the paint bright and new, and as miserably empty as her life seemed to be at that moment.

Logically, her mind told her that two places would have been almost perfect for her needs, but she hadn't been able to commit herself. She was unhappy, and half afraid that making an important decision in her present mood would put a shadow over her future.

She picked up a few things at the grocery store and drove home, tired and depressed. As she pulled into the drive and wearily got out of her own vehicle, she didn't notice the car sitting by the shrubbery across the street. She was halfway up the walk, her head down as she thought, when the sounds of hurrying footsteps caused her to look up. Adam Richfield was striding up the walk.

Suddenly all her fatigue seemed to fall away. After the initial shock of surprise, the logical part of her mind demanded protection and attempted to push objections to the forefront of her consciousness. Her heart twittered like a happy canary in the sunshine as she stood watching him, torn between delight and the pain of her decision.

He seemed as caught in cross-purpose as she. His

forceful, decisive striding stopped just four feet from her. He stood like a man late for an appointment who suddenly finds himself on the wrong floor of an office building. He took refuge in impatience.

'Where have you been? I started calling at five-thirty.'

'I'm just getting home,' Janet said unnecessarily. If he'd been calling, he knew that. She wasn't up to brilliant remarks at the moment. She noticed the bottle of champagne he carried. 'I hope that's to toast your first client. You'll be my first success.'

Her first success as well as his. Was she going to hear every detail? She felt unable to cope with it. But her job was to listen, aid, guide, encourage, and make happy sounds over his first steps towards a new life. She forcefully pulled her shoulders back and straightened herself to hear his news, but Adam had lost that decisiveness again.

He looked down at the bottle as if it were in the way. 'To launch a career,' he said. 'They launch ships that way, don't they?'

The fatigue of the past two weeks, the travel, the excitement of starting her own career, and the pain of her attempt to push Adam Richfield out of her life had brought on a mental exhaustion. The vision conjured up by his explanation for the champagne was literal. Her mind would not move past the visual image his words evoked.

'You want me to *hit* you with it?' Janet stared at him, her eyes wide, but no more so than his as he turned a startled look on her.

Then her reason took over. 'Of course not——' She raised her hand; on her arm her handbag dangled as she tried, by rubbing her hand across her face, to force away the cobwebs in her mind.

Adam's expression had gone through several changes

from amazement, suspicion and humour to a sudden tenderness. 'You've had a rough day,' he said, taking the grocery bag from her. 'Did you have any dinner?'

'I munched at a hamburger,' Janet told him as she led the way to the door, opened it with her key and flipped on the hall light.

Adam passed her, carrying the bag back to the kitchen.

Janet followed, watching him as he put the groceries on the counter, opened the hanging cabinets that formed a partial wall between the kitchen and the den and took out an ice bucket and two champagne glasses.

'You certainly cased this house thoroughly,' she said as she watched him. Why had that remark thrown him? she wondered.

He paused on his way to the refrigerator, his indrawn breath, his stance and his expression all seeming to prelude some earth-shaking confession. Then he seemed to think better of it and continued with the project of icing the champagne.

'If you're good at any job, you do it thoroughly,' he said. 'What's in the bag?' He put the ice bucket aside and explored Janet's purchases. 'Something tells me you don't cook,' he remarked, pulling out three packaged frozen dinners and two individual frozen pizzas.

'I do,' Janet stated flatly, her pride scored by his remarks. 'But I'm using a strange kitchen and I need time to find my own place. Harry Binns returns in two weeks——'

'Maybe he wouldn't object if you stayed,' said Adam. His mouth tightened as he made the suggestion.

Janet, putting her own connotation to his disapproval, turned indignant. 'I've never set eyes on Harry Binns!' She was adamant, almost shouting. 'And I assure you that neither my mother nor his is modern-minded enough to have had that in mind when——'

'Slow down, steamroller!' Adam interrupted. He took a firm grip on her shoulders. His eyes were soft, but his voice was commanding. 'You're exhausted. You're letting little things bother you.' His brows went up like an adult's condescension to a child. 'Turn on that oven,' he told her as he tore open the boxes holding the small individual pizzas. 'Then go plop on that sofa in the den.'

Janet wanted to follow his orders. She'd felt so alone that afternoon, and just having someone take that load of loneliness off her shoulders brought tears welling up. She felt the pain of strong emotion behind her brows. But logic reared its ugly head. Part of her problem had been trying to remove Adam Richfield from her life. She couldn't let him start managing her now.

But Adam had different ideas, and was ready to put them forcibly into action. He caught her by the arm and pulled her protesting into the den. Then he gently but firmly pushed her down on to the outer cushion of the big pit sofa, pulled off her heeled sandals, and pointed to the back of the sofa unit some six feet across the tufted cushions. 'Get back there and relax and look at the view. But before you go,' he caught her chin in his cupped hand and raised it to look in her eyes, 'I do have my first job.'

As he strode back to the kitchen, Janet sat where she was, nodding to the empty room. He would. She pushed away the vision of him sitting on the terrace of a restaurant overlooking the bay while some predatory female eyed him in the candlelight and laid plans for making him an exclusive offer.

Be professional, she warned herself, and wiggled her bare toes in the thick carpet and stood up. Perhaps the view and some fresh air would help her mood. She opened the glass doors that led to the terrace and went back to the pit sofa, kneeling on the outer cushion and crawling across it until she reached the back.

Not too good for the knees of her slacks, she decided as she tugged her clothes into place after her journey across the cushions. She had just seated herself, leaning against the back, when Adam came in carrying a tray.

'Pizza coming up shortly,' he said.

Janet twisted to watch him as he transferred the champagne glasses, the wine cooler and a stack of paper napkins from the tray to the narrow table that formed a wall round the pit sofa. 'Why didn't you say you had a customer already?' she said, trying to dredge up enthusiasm for his success even if she couldn't like the idea of another woman taking up his time.

He quirked an eyebrow at her, stepped towards the kitchen just far enough to put the tray on the counter dividing the two rooms, and walked round to the flat cushions of the pit sofa. Kicking off his shoes, he frowned, raised the legs of his trousers slightly, and crawled across the intervening cushions. When he'd covered the distance, he sat back on his knees, poured the champagne, and handed Janet the glass before he seated himself and leaned back. 'Here's to careers,' he said as he raised his glass.

They touched glasses, each took a swallow, then Janet raised her glass again.

'To your first customer,' she said.

'I'll drink to that.'

They clicked glasses and drank again.

But when he lowered his, his eyes were creased with laughter. 'But I said job, not customer.'

'What's the difference?' asked Janet, puzzled that he should differentiate between the two.

'Are you paying?' His smile widened.

'Me?' She was more confused than ever. 'I don't understand. I'm not——'

'Familiar with the town,' Adam said, interrupting her at the precise moment to make his point. 'I am. Not all apartments are listed in the papers. Tomorrow I'll take you on a tour of several neighbourhoods.'

'Well, thank you, but I don't know.' She wasn't sure how to answer him.

'My work takes me everywhere——' he paused in mid-sentence. 'I know the area,' he finished quickly.

Janet smiled and took another sip from her glass, thinking he was a fast learner. Two nights before she'd warned him to stop thinking in reference to his criminal career, and he was certainly trying. His deliberate switch and the irritated frown showed he'd been slightly angry with himself for slipping even once. She admired his determination.

In the kitchen, a single ding of a bell startled them both.

Adam reached behind him to set his glass on the narrow table. 'Dinner's ready. No, you stay. I'll get it. When it comes to frozen food that slides on to paper plates, I'm a *chef extraordinaire*.'

He'd crawled halfway to the edge of the cushioned square when he stopped, twisted his body slightly and looked back over his shoulder at her. With one hand he patted the cushion. 'Give me a female opinion. Do you think this thing's romantic?'

'Well——' Janet hedged. She really didn't want to get on the subject of romance.

'I don't,' he grumbled. 'I don't see a thing titillating about crawling around with your behind up in the air.'

Janet, who'd just taken another sip of champagne, choked. She was holding a napkin to her mouth as he stood up and looked back at her.

'Will you live?' he asked.

Still caught between laughing and coughing, she nodded and he continued into the kitchen.

Once her spasms were under control, she finished the champagne and set her glass behind her on the table.

She stretched luxuriously, enjoying the softness of the sofa, turning her foot to rub it against the velvet pile. Outside the window, the lights on the hills of San Diego were like piles of jewels.

Funny, she thought, how much brighter they looked when she and Adam shared the view. The memories of her day's misery tried to intrude; the logic that had caused her to decide to drop Adam Richfield out of her life was still sound. The view, the soft breeze weaving its way in through the open doors, the lassitude of her fatigue and the champagne, the smell of pizza in the kitchen, and the enjoyment of Adam Richfield's company demanded precedence over good sense.

In moments he returned, leaning over the back of the sofa as he handed her the woven straw holders which held paper plates and the two small pizzas cut into manageable slices.

'Ah ha! You got ahead of me,' he said.

She heard the tinkling of the ice as he pulled out the champagne bottle and filled the glasses before going round to the end of the sofa and crawling across again.

Janet sat holding the two plates, savouring the aroma of the pizzas. She watched him as he crawled up beside her and turned, leaning back against the cushions. He stretched his long legs out across the expanse of the unit.

His eyes met hers as he turned to take one of the plates and seemed to hold her entrapped in his gaze. 'I think I'm going to say something personal,' he said softly.

Even through the clouding effects of the champagne, the logical part of Janet's mind warned her to take care. But she wasn't listening. 'Just how personal?' she murmured, handing him his plate and watching him slide his fingers carefully under one of the small slices.

'Very personal,' he said, picking up the slice of pizza. 'Time to feed your face.'

She wasn't sure whether she was relieved or disappointed. But she couldn't prevent a chuckle. 'I'm beginning to think you chose the wrong business,' she said.

His response was a questioning 'Ummph?' caused by having a mouthful of pizza.

'Umm-hmmm,' she answered him with an equally inarticulate sound, nodding her head for emphasis while she swallowed a savoury bite of cheese, crust and sausage. She took another sip of champagne to wash it down. 'You do get practical at the strangest times.'

'I'll watch that in the future,' he said.

A few minutes later, the straw holders and paper plates perched empty and ignored on the narrow table surrounding the sofa and Janet and Adam sat leaning back, each holding a glass containing the last of the champagne. Janet let her head fall back on the cushions and turned slightly, as through partially closed lids she surveyed Adam, who was no more than a silhouette against the light of the kitchen.

'Something's happened to my bones,' she said. 'I have this amazing picture of myself not being able to walk. Just slithering off the sofa and across the floor.'

'It's champagne,' Adam answered. 'It dissolves everything.'

'Umm-hmm,' said Janet. 'I notice you go in for all these disintegrating things like Scotch, weird stuff sold in flowerpots, and champagne. I have this vague suspicion that you're trying to get me loaded again.'

'Now why should I do that?'

'I haven't the foggiest idea,' she said. 'Oh, I know why you did on Monday night. You wanted to mellow my mood so that I wouldn't call the cops.'

'Well, you should have figured out tonight too, Adam retorted. 'I'm out to seduce you. After all, I put this playpen here for exactly that reason.'

'Well, maybe you didn't, but Harry Binns probably had something similar in mind,' she said. Then her eyes opened and she lifted her head. 'Playpen?'

'That's what they call them.'

Janet frowned at the pit sofa. The nickname should not have added to the mood, but it made her slightly uncomfortable, as though in sitting on it she was giving a tacit agreement to an involvement she was not emotionally prepared to allow herself.

'Playpen,' she murmured. 'Somehow I can't imagine it full of baby rattles and rubber ducks.'

Adam chuckled. 'No, I think it's the kind you fill with beautiful dolls. Dolls that walk and talk——' He suited that action by taking two fingers of his right hand and walking them down the back of Janet's forearm. 'Smooth, soft and silky dolls,' he said softly.

His voice had turned husky, penetrating beyond words in their meanings, reaching past logic and touching the inner chords that strummed in her emotions. His walking fingers left tiny points of sensation on her skin, and Janet, looking down at her arm, wouldn't have been surprised to see some visual mark of his touch.

Caught off base by this sudden switch in mood, she strove to bring the conversation back to its former lightness. 'And wooden soldiers?' she asked with a smile.

'No, not wooden,' Adam's huskiness had deepened. His fingers ceased their walk and closed round her wrist, forming a soft warm band of sensation. His hand moved up her arm and on to her shoulder.

Janet, her eyes wide, stared at him. She was getting into deeper trouble, she told herself, but his touch as his hand moved on to the skin at the back of her neck was creating fiery sensations within her, melting away all her resistance.

He raised his head, turning it slightly, and brought his lips down on hers. Gently. A warmth of touch. The teasing lightness gave promise of delights just out of reach.

His feathered teasing had moved from her lips on to her cheek, awakening her flesh to new moods. A nerve twitched beneath the skin. Without conscious orders her arms came up around him, drawing him closer, demanding that he should fulfil the promise of his teasing.

His lips came back to hers. His hunger branded new sensations into her skin. One hand was behind her head, his other arm slipped under her hips and he turned her body. Together they rolled across the cushions of the sofa pit, stretching full-length on the velvet softness. Janet clung to him. Her hands caressed his back, too hungry for his kiss, his touch, to allow even a moment's separation.

As he laid her on the pillowed softness, his hard body pressed on hers. His chest, his thighs, the force of his masculinity bruised her flesh, her senses. Her hands, on his back, encountered the silk shirt, pulled at it, resenting its interference that kept her from caressing his skin, from giving to him the same sensations of delight that were affecting her. Her lips were still clinging to his as she tugged ineffectually at the tail of his shirt. He moved, the weight of his body lifting off hers as he shifted.

In that small movement, Janet's world seemed to shift. Then Adam was gone. Disappeared.

She lay on her back, staring at the ceiling, in total shock and gasping for breath. Not sure what had happened, she wondered if she had been suddenly awakened from a vivid dream. No reality seemed to fit her screaming senses.

'Damn!' A muffled voice came from beside and below her.

She turned her head and stared at the black void that split the pit sofa.

Adam's head came into view. He sat up slowly, cramped by the tight space left by the shifting of the ottomans.

Every nerve in Janet's body screamed outrage, but as she stared at Adam, whose own chagrin and shock had brought his sensuous lips out in a small-boy pout, she couldn't hold back the laughter threatening to tear her apart if she prevented it from escaping.

'I don't think it's *that* funny!' Adam retorted as he struggled to get up off the floor, hampered by the narrow space.

Janet sat up and held out a hand, though she couldn't stop laughing.

'No, thank you.' He drew back, and by pushing against the other cushions created enough space to get to his knees and on to his feet. 'I told you this thing wasn't romantic!' He stared down at the pit sofa as if he expected it to go rolling off across the room.

Janet watched as he sat gingerly on an ottoman and swung his legs over to reach the floor. He reached down, and she could tell by his movements that he was putting on his shoes. Feeling a sense of loss, she crept to the edge, now, like him, slightly nervous, fearing a sudden movement would cause her to fall.

'I'm sorry,' she said as she reached the edge and looked for her sandals. 'I shouldn't have laughed.'

'You shouldn't,' his voice was haughty, but he was fighting back laughter too. 'Just for that, I'll push this monster back into place and you can clean up.'

He moved his hand to indicate the glasses and plates still on the long narrow table behind the back of the sofa. Once he'd pushed the ottomans back into place, he caught Janet's hand and led her to the kitchen, where he removed his coat which he'd hung on the knob of a counter door. Then he led her towards the front hall.

Janet, still caught up in an emotional loss, stood silent while he draped the coat round her shoulders and pulled her close. 'Eleven o'clock in the morning,' he said, the authority in his voice brooking no objections. 'I'll pick you up. We'll look at a couple of places and have lunch.'

She nodded. And as he exerted pressure on the arms of the coat he held round her shoulders, she allowed herself to be pulled forward until his lips touched hers. Though her arms ached to hold him, she kept them at her side. His were drawn behind him as he used the coat to hold her tantalisingly close, though torturously too far away for their bodies to touch. As his lips left hers, he eased the pressure on the garment and slightly increased the distance between them.

'Just one thing,' he said softly.

'Umm-hmm?'

'If you put a pit sofa in your living-room, I'll burn down the building.'

The silk jacket slid round her as he freed one arm and, catching the coat up, opened the door.

After Janet had locked it behind him, she returned to the den and carried the glasses, ice bucket and dishes back into the kitchen. She tried to concentrate on the mundane acts of washing the champagne glasses and emptying and drying the ice bucket, but her thoughts kept returning to Adam.

She glanced through the racks of sparkling glasses to the soft light of the den, where the pile of the playpen's velvet depths pulled at her senses. She should be thankful the recalcitrant ottomans chose to slip apart at that moment. She wasn't. The last thing she wanted was to be involved with a man who could end up in jail at any minute. That was a lie. At eleven the next morning, she'd thank him very civilly for his offer to assist her in finding an apartment. She didn't require any assistance, and she'd tell him so.

Would she?

She would.

Oh yeah?

I will!

Still fighting the battle, Janet turned off the lights and headed for the bedroom.

CHAPTER SIX

As Adam walked through the back door of the office, his footsteps echoed with that particular hollowness of a building empty of people. Occasionally a few of the staff worked overtime and would be in at the weekend, but at the moment all the jobs in hand were running smoothly and on schedule. He'd expected total silence when he came into the office that morning.

The gurgle-blurp of the coffee pot warned him that someone else was in the building. He checked the doors of the survey room and the architectural department and found them both locked, but a little way up the hall the door to the main drafting rooms of the engineering department stood ajar. He pushed it open to see Rhoda wearing jeans, boots, a denim jacket and an old cowboy hat. She was leaning across a desk looking at a plan sheet.

'Riding out on the lone prairie?' he asked, though he recognised her clothing as her field uniform.

She looked up at him, a slight frown on her chubby features. 'Something's wrong,' she said, turning back to the drawing. 'These contours just don't fit my picture of that lot over on Forty-eighth and Jackson.'

Adam walked over and stared down at the drawing. The series of gradually curving lines meandering across a drawing of a corner lot would have been incomprehensible to anyone not familiar with civil engineering. But to Adam and Rhoda, with years of experience in the field, they spoke a language of sloping banks gradually levelling into a flatter slope here and there gorged with small gullies.

Adam had given the property a cursory inspection when he bid for the job, but some last-minute problem with finances had prevented the design work from being started for almost two years. He no longer remembered the property.

'What's bothering you?' he asked her, waiting while she frowned and chewed on her lip.

'I don't know. I'm not sure that anything's wrong. I just don't feel right about it and I want to check it out.'

Adam looked down at his watch. He had three hours before he was due to pick up Janet and take her apartment-hunting. The property was less than ten minutes away from the office, and he did remember it well enough to know they could check a few details without stepping off the pavement.

'If I go out there with you, you're going to do the measuring' he told Rhoda. 'I've just put a shine on these boots.'

'Heavy date this morning?' asked Rhoda as she rolled up the drawing and picked up the survey book.

'Just mind your own business,' Adam said. 'You fill a Thermos with coffee. I'll put some equipment in a truck.'

While he loaded a transit, a tape, a surveyor's rod and an extendable rod, Rhoda filled the Thermos and locked the engineering room and the back door. She climbed in the passenger side of the survey van as Adam started the engine.

They were a block away from the office when he took his eyes off the street long enough to give Rhoda an appraising glance. 'You're an apartment liver, aren't you?'

She pushed her felt hat back on her head. 'I'm a liver no matter where I am.'

'No, I mean you know what's available.'

She looked interested. 'For who? Are you thinking of moving?'

Adam shook his head as he gave a signal and concentrated on turning a corner.

Rhoda correctly surmised his interest in an apartment. 'Janet Talbot's thinking of moving.'

'Why don't you just answer the question?' Adam demanded.

But Rhoda was on the scent and wouldn't leave it. 'You must have talked ver—ry pretty last night if she accepted your story and will still let you help her find an apartment.'

Adam didn't answer.

Rhoda wasn't stupid. 'You didn't tell her.'

'She was just too tired,' Adam said, attempting to shrug off the implications of not having told Janet the truth. He divided his attention between his driving and the chubby woman in the passenger side of the truck.

That satisfied smile on his project manager's face was sending his temper from placid up the scale towards dangerous.

'I'll *tell* her!' he said.

'You won't,' Rhoda was little-girl-pleased and prim at the same time. The way her eyes danced, Adam halfway expected her to start some silly sing-song chatter, *Boss has got a girl-friend. Nyah, nyah, nyah.*

'I'm going to tell her today!' His irritated insistence was caused as much by his own lack of action as by Rhoda's attitude.

'I will say no more,' said Rhoda, turning haughty. But her eyes kept laughing at him.

'I'll tell her,' Adam insisted.

'Of course you will.'

'I will!'

'I *believe* you.'

'I mean it.'

'You *mean* it,' Rhoda agreed, her voice carrying a disgusting amiable disbelief.

Adam pulled the truck over to the kerb as he reached the corner of the property they'd come to inspect. He put the gear-lever in park and pushed his foot down hard on the emergency brake pedal. 'If you're going to argue, argue. If you're not, shut up.'

Still with unimpaired amiability, Rhoda nodded, her mouth closed.

Adam's anger caused him to slam the door of the survey van as he stepped out into the street. But when Rhoda climbed out and unrolled the plans she carried, they were both all business again.

The legal divisions from a subdivision map recorded in 1925 split the large vacant area into four city lots. Two had always been vacant. An old house had been condemned and pulled down on one property. On the lot nearest the corner another had burned, and the debris had been carried away years before. Now zoned commercial, it was to be the location of a medical building.

While Adam held the left side of the two-by-three-foot plan sheet, Rhoda held the right.

'Missed that telephone pole,' Adam said, using a nod of his head for a direction indicator as he looked from the property to the plan and back again.

'And there's not one on this side!—oh, good God!'

As Rhoda saw the problem, it also occurred to Adam and he started to laugh.

After her initial shock, Rhoda was laughing too. 'I don't believe it. I thought Ames was past this.'

Able to read the contours and accurately judge the property in front of them, it was easy to tell what had happened. The tracing had been put on backwards.

Adam's mouth quirked on one side as he smiled, remembering his own first inexperienced days on the drafting board. He'd once made a similar error with less cause. The property in front of them was nearly square and bounded on three sides by streets. The countour lines showing the elevations across the property had been carefully plotted. And the blueprint copy had been made to insure against the loss of the work.

Blueprint machines are notorious traps for beginners. The copies are made by strong light burning away a treated surface and leaving only those areas covered by pencilled or inked linework. The machines weren't particular about whether a drawing was put in right-side-up or upside-down. The draughtsman had some-how put his print in the machine incorrectly while making his print, and had very carefully traced it on the master drawing backwards.

While Rhoda was still staring at the print, Adam's grin turned sly. Then he carefully hid it. He had a chance to throw Rhoda off stride, and he wasn't about to let the opportunity pass.

'And you wanted me to give this guy a raise.'

Her head jerked up as she stared at him outraged. 'It can happen to anybody. Look how square this property is. The sidewalks have exactly the same radii at both corners . . .'

Adam strove to hold a severe judgemental expression while Rhoda hotly defended her new draughtsman until he tired of the joke. He pointed down the street to a red and orange sign that advertised the location of a restaurant chain.

'Let's go and have breakfast and talk it over.'

'I've already had breakfast,' said Rhoda, refusing to be mollified.

Expecting to outrage her all the more, he reached down and gave her a light slap where her heavy thighs threatened to split the denim of her jeans. 'Looks as if you've got room for a second one,' he said.

Rhoda viewed the excess weight of her hips and thighs with a dissatisfaction that had become commonplace. 'Always. That's the problem. But you're not going to take this out on Ames, are you?'

'I'll put you both on probation,' Adam said, turning back to the truck. 'I never have been sure if you're going to work out on the job either.'

Pacified by his teasing, Rhoda rolled up the plan and climbed back into the truck. It wasn't until they were in the restaurant giving most of their attention to plates of bacon and eggs that Rhoda brought up the subject of Janet again.

'Why don't you admit it? You don't want to tell her.'

'I'm going to tell her,' Adam growled. He pointed his fork at her as he reiterated his decision. 'I'm going to tell her *today*.'

'I'm going to tell him today,' Janet threatened her reflection in the bathroom mirror by shaking her finger at it. 'And this time I'm going to make it stick.'

She had told him before that she wouldn't continue to see him. No, she hadn't exactly put it in those terms. She had told him he no longer needed her help, so maybe she hadn't made it plain. She'd make her point clearer.

She couldn't tell Adam Richfield how important he was likely to become in her life. Or, because of her growing feeling for him, the danger he represented. A sense of preservation warned her to keep her vulnerabilities to herself. She had to remain the professional. More professional than she had been the night before, she decided, remembering with embarrassment how willing she had been to accept his lovemaking. Her senses had been outraged when that ridiculous accident of his falling between the ottomans had saved her from taking a giant step into an impossible relationship.

Her weakness the night before had been the result of

her fatigue, she decided, and knew she was lying to herself.

'Don't kid yourself,' she argued with the mirror. 'When your bones turn to water every time you look at him, that's not fatigue, that's *heart* trouble.'

Impatiently she gathered up the cosmetics spread on the countertop, crammed them in the little plastic bag and returned to the bedroom to finish dressing. She'd meet him at the door, thank him for coming, and tell him she should do her apartment-hunting alone.

Her watch said a quarter to eleven. She hurried as she slipped into a pair of sandals and a pale blue linen dress. Too fast, she decided, as she raised the skirt of the dress and smoothed the slip beneath it. She was behaving with the harum-scarum rush that characterised a date.

'I'm not going on a date,' she kept telling herself. 'I'm not even going with Adam Richfield. I'm going apartment-hunting. I'm going alone!'

'I'm going alone,' she said as Adam took her arm and guided her towards his car.

She'd left her handbag, her folded newspaper and her map on the hall table by the front door. And, true to her plan, she had thanked Adam for coming when he arrived at five minutes before eleven. She told him she felt struggling with a map would help her learn about the city.

The door had been open, and while he listened he looked beyond her into the hall. He had seen her map, the newspaper and bag, and by the simple expedient of picking them up with one hand and catching her arm with the other, had ushered her out towards his car.

'I need to learn the city on my *own*!' Janet was insisting as he released her hand long enough to open the car door and then, with gentle pressure, put her inside.

'You can learn it on your own,' Adam answered with

a humorous patience. 'You pick out an area, take your map and navigate. I'll turn when you tell me.'

'That's not the same thing,' Janet said.

'Show me the difference as we go,' he answered with imperturbable good humour as he closed the car door.

It wasn't until he started back down the walk towards the house that Janet became aware they'd left the front door standing open. Once it was locked and he came back again, taking his seat behind the wheel, she glared at him.

'All right, pick an address.'

'I don't pick an address. I pick a price!' Janet corrected him. 'Then I work it out from there.' She looked up and down the folded newspaper with likely advertisements highlighted in yellow, and fingered one. 'How about this one?'

Adam looked at it and grinned. 'Do you want to work out the route on the map?'

'No. If I'm going to be chauffeured I'll take all the conveniences,' Janet said, still irritated at being overridden.

Adam nodded, started the car and pulled it away from the kerb.

She watched him as he drove. His hands, so capable on the steering wheel, seemed to be acting apart from his mind. He appeared to be absorbed in serious thought, and since she could hardly spend all their time together repeating her decision to break off this new relationship she was willing to sit quietly.

After a few minutes of silence, he reached over and pushed the button on the tape deck. She was pleasantly surprised to hear the beginning notes of Wagner's *Parsifal*. The force of the music fitted Adam's personality, she thought.

Unwilling to allow her mind to dwell exclusively on the man behind the wheel, Janet watched the passing scene. They were driving through an old subdivision, she decided. The houses had basic similarities in shapes, white stucco walls and red Spanish tile roofs. But additions through the years, the variation of shrubbery and flowers, the lavish use of bougainvillaea climbing archways and carports, gave each house its own personality. Maybe there was even hope for the new, more modern subdivisions where the homes appeared to be cranked out on some gigantic assembly line, she thought.

Her mind was pulled away from the subdivision as Adam swung on to a cloverleaf ramp and they came out on a wide freeway. Janet was unused to freeways and they made her nervous. She became absorbed in watching the behaviour of the drivers of other vehicles. But after a few minutes she realised the distance they were travelling.

'Where is this place?' she asked, a little puzzled that they were moving at a speed a little less than a mile a minute and travelling up a valley bounded on both sides by enormous hills on top of which she could see clusters of houses. They were just starting up a long slow grade when she asked her question.

'You're in Mission Valley,' Adam told her.

'But it seems to me we're getting a good way from where I'll be working. Exactly where is this Carlton Oaks?'

'It's in Santee. Only about fifteen miles from where we are now,' he said with a half-smile.

'But I don't want to be that far away!' Janet objected.

'Express your desire and it will be done,' said Adam.

She sat fuming for a moment and then sighed. A capitulation to defeat. 'I suppose I do need help. I want to be downtown. I've never lived in a big city, and I'd like to feel I'm in the midst of things. I suppose I'd better listen to your advice.' She begrudged the concession, but common sense seemed to leave her no alternative.

Her reward was a smile from Adam, who gave a signal, moved into the right lane and took the nearest exit. With very little trouble they crossed a bridge over the freeway, took another cloverleaf ramp, and were speeding back in the direction they'd come.

His continued silence began to irritate her.

'Anyone can make a mistake,' she said, her voice short and clipped. She didn't consider it very thoughtful of him or very gallant to appear as though he was thoroughly enjoying her error. But the look he gave her was cryptic. No more so than his remarks that followed.

'Anyone can make a wrong turn. Happens in the best of families.'

'Mine was made out of ignorance,' Janet snapped. 'After all, I didn't pretend to know the city.'

'Ignorance of a place or a circumstance. It can be the same thing,' Adam answered.

She wasn't quite sure what he meant and was a little bothered, feeling she had missed a double meaning. 'Would you like to elaborate?' she said.

He looked slightly uncomfortable. Then, by the deep breath he took before speaking, she felt as if he was plunging into deep water.

Cold water.

'It's not necessarily routes on a map. People make wrong turns in their lives——' He paused as he changed lanes, moving to the right to take another freeway, 163 according to the large signs stretched across the six lanes. 'They putter along, and then some circumstance takes them off on a detour and the next thing you know, they're caught up in a mess.'

He was going to tell her he was involved in some new criminal activity, she decided. She couldn't listen. it would be Derek all over again. Fate just didn't play fair.

She took a deep breath, plunging into waters chillingly cold and hoping she could shock him back to his senses.

'Routes and maps are not quite like lives,' she said. 'While a person may get confused on the location of a street, any sensible individual knows well in advance the possible result of his actions.'

Adam bit his lip. His eyes remained on the road. 'You won't concede that some thoughtless action, one that lands a person in a mess, could be overlooked?'

She did, but decided against admitting it and perhaps giving tacit approval or at least condonement for some illegal action on his part. 'I do not. I'll amend that. Perhaps in a child or a person of limited mentality, but if you're speaking of you or me—no.'

He sighed. 'Then let's drop the subject.'

For a few minutes the air was loaded with tension. They rode in silence until they had left the freeway, and after several turns they reached a large park. He brought the car to halt at the kerb under a large shade tree.

By his attitude, he had wiped the previous conversation from his mind. 'Let me see your map,' he requested. She handed it over. With a few expert flips he opened it to the area he desired, and after checking the scale in the corner, folded it to a manageable size. Pulling a pen from his pocket, he made an X on the map. 'This is where you work,' he said. 'Now, ideally, how close would you like to be to the job?'

'Within two miles,' Janet said positively. At his flicker of interest, she elaborated. 'Suppose the car breaks down, or we have another gas emergency? I should be able to walk.'

Adam nodded, then using his thumb and forefinger he measured off the distance and drew a light circle on the map. While he was at it, he made three more circles, labelling them 2, 3, 4 and 5. 'There's a basic difference between the places you'll see in this area and further out. The buildings downtown are older. The rooms may be larger——'

'They probably have more individual character,' Janet added. She loved old buildings.

Adam nodded. 'But most of them were built at a time before swimming pools and jacuzzis became a necessary part of apartment living. Further out, you find pools——'

'With the ocean this close?' Janet asked wide-eyed. 'I'm not interested in a pool.'

Adam grinned, and she wondered for a moment if he was laughing at her mid-Western enthusiasm. But he took another pen from his pocket and handed it to her, then tapped the newspaper lying in her lap. 'You read out an address, I'll locate it on the map, and if it's within a reasonable distance we'll mark it with a number. We'll get some organisation into this search.'

Both their attitudes turned businesslike as Janet read out addresses. Adam checked the map and gave her the general idea of the location.

Half an hour later, Janet sighed despondently. 'I never knew there were so many apartments and so *many* of them so far away.'

Adam looked up and smiled. 'San Diego and its environs cover over seven hundred square miles,' he said, tapping the newspaper she held. 'Don't fret. You have five more pages to go.'

'And they're such *big* pages,' said Janet, looking at the paper.

'We found four in the immediate area,' Adam said, consulting the map. 'And I think you're tired of this.'

For the third time, her gaze had wandered out across the park toward a hot dog stand. The red and white awning, the stainless steel bins that steamed the rolls and the hot dogs, and the white-uniformed man who was at present handing over two Cokes to a child about ten years old were reminiscent of her own childhood.

'I can't help it,' her voice was plaintive. 'There's just something *wonderful* about hot dogs in the park.'

Adam had trouble keeping his face straight. Then, with a sudden move, he tossed the map into the back seat. 'I guess we'd better take care of the emergency first,' he said, opening the car door and walking round to her side.

Janet won the battle with her appetite and restricted herself to one hot dog. But Adam ordered two for himself.

'If we snitch *all* his napkins, we can have chili and onions too,' he suggested to Janet as he gave the order.

Feeling like a little kid again, she followed Adam to a bench in the shade of a tree and they sat eating and drinking while the breeze stirred the leaves of the trees above them and the smell of newly cut grass drifted up from their feet.

'Very grown up and dignified,' muttered Adam, when he caught Janet licking the mustard off her fingers.

'Look who's talking,' she countered, pointing the rest of the hot dog at the two he held.

'Don't point things at me.' He drew back. 'You make me think you're hiding a gun in that wrapper.'

She laughed, thinking about the Monday night when she'd pointed the weapon at him. 'I can't believe I did that,' she admitted. 'It's a wonder you didn't take it away from me.'

'Are you kidding? I was afraid you'd pull that trigger.'

'Did I really look as if I knew how to handle it?' The idea pleased her.

'Enough to fool me. You mean you bought that gun with no idea how to use it?'

'I didn't *buy* it,' Janet said, nibbling on her hot dog. 'Mother took one of Dad's and hid it in my suitcase. I didn't know I had it until I unpacked at Harry's.'

'You brought it across country in your suitcase?'

She nodded absently, concentrating on licking the last of the chili off the paper wrapper before crushing it. 'If Mother hadn't had the foresight to put it in a plastic bag, it would have ruined my lingerie.'

'Baw!'

The demanding little voice behind her caused her to turn. A chubby two-year-old stood pointing a fist in the general direction of the ground beneath the bench. Janet looked down to see a red, white and blue rubber ball lying by her feet. She picked it up.

'Is this your ball?'

'Baw,' the infant affirmed, and hurried round the bench, his small feet moving with the unbelievable speed peculiar to children of his age.

The toy was some eight inches in diameter, the colours sparkling fresh, and it boasted its newness by the small square price tag still stuck on it. The little boy took it carefully and showed it to Adam. 'Baw'. His description, if superfluous, was at least brief.

'Yes.' Adam seemed to give the sphere due consideration. 'I'd nearly reached that conclusion myself.'

The child viewed the pair on the bench, a careful wide-eyed scrutiny, handed the ball back to Janet, and climbed up on the bench between them. Janet moved over, picking up her soda to keep it from being overturned.

'Now what?' muttered Adam as he slid to the side so that the child could wriggle around, settling himself. His chubby legs stuck out over the edge of the bench. Then he leaned forward, his attention fixed on Adam's remaining hot dog.

'Now what do I do?' Adam eyed the child warily.

'You don't mess with people's kids,' he said, turning to look for a stray parent.

Adam's view was blocked by the tree that provided the shade for the bench, but Janet, twisting round, saw an elderly woman with a cane. She was hurrying in their direction, impeded by a limp.

'Help is on the way. Oh, dear!' While she was watching the woman, the toddler had lifted the soda from her relaxed hand and was gulping it down.

'He *took* it!' Janet said, not sure how to get it back.

Adam grinned. 'He'd make a great little thief.'

'Don't start recruiting!' She stared at the child, not sure what to do. Visions of hungry children flitted through her mind, but they didn't fit the child who sat between them. He was chubby, bright-eyed and pink-cheeked. Like his toy, his clothes were new or nearly so. The logo on his shirt was recognisable from television commercials.

The elderly woman who limped round the end of the bench was also well-dressed. She arrived just as Janet attempted to retrieve the paper cup. But when she reached for it, the child drew back.

'No!' he protested, sloshing the soda as he gulped.

'Ricky!' The woman was scandalised. 'Oh, I'm so sorry,' she apologised.

'Eat,' Ricky announced, and giving Janet back the empty cup he reached for Adam's hot dog.

'Not this one, friend,' Adam held it out of reach. 'You wouldn't like chili and onions.'

'Wa-nt,' Ricky told him. His tone said he was being reasonable, and Adam should follow his example.

'Ricky, you can't take people's food,' the grey-haired woman admonished the child. She tried to take his hand to remove him from the bench, but the toddler drew back and shook his head obstinately. She seemed to be at as much of a loss as Janet and Adam, and Janet could tell she was genuinely uncomfortable.

'I'm so sorry. He's too young to understand.'

Adam rose nobly to the occasion and to his feet. 'Would you be our guest for lunch?' he asked the lady with a smile. 'Gourmet hot dogs and—I think—milk?'

'Muk,' Ricky agreed, turning an angelic smile on Adam.

While Adam sauntered back to the hot dog stand, Janet accepted Miss Graham's apologies. She was a great-aunt who'd never had children of her own, she told Janet. Ricky's mother was at the moment in hospital and had that morning given the toddler a baby sister.

'And if I live through Wednesday, his next visit will be when he's twenty-one.'

'He's a darling boy,' Janet temporised.

Ricky climbed down from the bench. Before Janet could catch him, he was toddling after Adam.

'He's a *marvellous* child,' Miss Graham sighed. 'And he'll be a great success in life. He always knows exactly what he wants.'

He did. After he'd eaten half his hot dog, drunk as much of his milk as he cared to and poured the rest of it on the ground, he wanted Janet to play ball.

Though she'd risen from the bench reluctantly, she found a release in chasing Ricky's enthusiastic but erratic tosses. The physical exertion eased her tension, and for a while she forgot the nervousness of starting a new job, the lack of having her own place to live in and the conflict that accompanied her thoughts about Adam Richfield. Little Ricky's innocent demands to be entertained and his pleasure at having someone chase the wild tosses of his ball were just the release she needed.

When the toddler had run his fill and his chubby little legs had become unsteady with fatigue, Janet picked up the ball and the child and went back to the bench, where Adam and Miss Graham were relaxing in the shade.

'Playtime over?' asked Adam with a slow, lazy smile.

'We've climbed Mount Everest, right there,' Janet pointed to the sunny expanse of the lawn where she had played with the child. 'And *I* feel it!'

Her skin prickled with heat. The dry breeze, playing through her hair, was sharply cool on her skin.

'I'd say you wore out your companion,' said Adam, glancing down at Ricky, who was drifting off to sleep now that he was still. 'Why don't we see Miss Graham home? I'll carry the little monster.'

Janet agreed and rose, giving him room to gather up the dozing child and settle the little fellow in his arms. She noticed the unsurprised acceptance of Miss Graham, and decided the elderly woman and Adam had come to some arrangement on the subject before Janet had returned to the bench. It was kind of him, she thought. The little crippled woman would have had trouble trying to take a sleepy protesting child across the busy street. Janet doubted very much if Miss Graham could have carried Ricky.

Allowing herself to be moved along by the tide of the others' plans, Janet strolled behind them admiring the large old houses that faced across the street into the park. They turned into the driveway by the side of a big, pale-blue Victorian house and walked down the slope of the driveway.

'. . . and since I can't do much with the steps any more, I took the bottom floor for my use and turned the rest of the house into apartments.'

At the mention of apartments, Janet's attention snapped back to her companions. Her eyes travelled up the side of the building, viewing the windows above. Hope that Miss Graham might have something available quickly faded as she saw the open windows, giving evidence that the building was fully occupied.

The park was well within the two-mile radius of what she would like, and she threw a wistful look at a vine of particularly brilliant bougainvillaea that created a bright red arch over a doorway leading into a large garage at the back of the house. It had been a carriage house in another day, Janet thought, and allowed her imagination to create the vision of a delicate four-wheeled vehicle with plush-upholstered seats in the back, a high perch for a driver and two spirited horses, their harnesses topped with plumes.

'Coming?' Adam's voice intruded into her reverie, and Janet hurried up the three steps to the side entrance to the lower floor of the main house.

She stepped into a sunny room and tried to classify it—a delightful hodge-podge she loosely termed a parlour-den. The furniture, mostly antique, was mixed with bright cushions, shining brass lamps and bowls. And by a comfortable rocker, situated so that it faced a large television, was a wicker basket in the shape of a frog, and sticking out of its mouth were a pair of knitting needles worked into what appeared to be a portion of a sweater. Obviously Miss Graham combined the best of both her girlhood and the modern world with a charming disregard for style.

From the hall she could hear the hushed voices of Adam and Miss Graham and their approaching footsteps as the elderly lady entered the room, followed by Adam. She was jingling a set of keys in her hand. She stopped in the middle of the floor and handed them to Adam with a bright-eyed look at Janet.

He was also smiling. 'Have you ever thought of living in an outhouse?' he asked her.

'A what?' queried Janet, a litle surprised.

'A carriage house,' Miss Graham corrected him, her eyes lively with humour. 'I'll let you two take a look while I put on a pot of tea.'

Janet was so surprised that she followed Adam out of the door and down the drive without either protest or excitement. The thought of arriving home in the evenings and being welcomed to her door by that arch of brilliant red flowers seemed too good to be true. The area was so beautiful, the park close at hand, and the location so exactly fitted her needs. Janet steeled herself, fearing something must be wrong. When she'd been circling ads in the paper, Adam had been peering over her shoulder, but perhaps he had not noticed the monthly rental range that she considered her limit.

They walked into the living-room and Janet's heart gave a lurch. Gorgeous. The large windows threw the light on a dusty, polished wooden floor and lit the rafters a good eighteen feet above her head. To her left, a stairway rose to connect with a balcony that formed a landing off which four doors opened.

'Bedrooms upstairs,' Adam grinned, and led the way to an arched opening beneath the rising stair. Janet followed, passing through an informal dining-area and into a well-appointed kitchen. 'No dishwasher,' Adam observed.

'Forget the dishwasher,' she said, admiring the gleaming but dusty countertops and the abundance of cabinet space. 'Just get me out of here. I can't afford this.'

But her desire caused her to pause and open a small door to find a half-bath. Like the rest of the apartment, dusty but with modern fixtures and shining tile.

'Let's peek upstairs,' said Adam, and led the way.

Janet paused at the foot of the stairway, hardly daring to climb. What those four doors meant she had no idea, and wondered if she dared look. She followed him slowly, to look into two large, light bedrooms, a well-appointed bath, and a smaller storage room.

'This is gorgeous,' she said again. 'But take me out of here. It's going to be far beyond my price range.'

When Adam named the monthly rent Janet stared at him, disbelieving. Her eyes narrowed slightly.

'What's wrong with it?' She'd stepped back out on to the balconied passage and stood looking wistfully down on the large living-room below her. Nothing was wrong with the apartment, she knew. Her good luck was too good. She still questioned it.

'How did you arrange it?' she asked. Still slightly suspicious, she looked up at Adam.

'I didn't,' he said. 'I think you swung it by playing with Ricky. Look around you.' With the toe of his rubber-soled shoe, he rubbed his foot across the floor exposing the gleam of a perfect finish beneath the dust. 'She hasn't rented this place lately—if ever. I got the impression she doesn't care if it sits empty—she just liked *you*.'

Forty-five minutes later, and fortified with herb tea, they left Miss Graham's house, crossed the street, entered the park again and were on their way back to Harry Binns' house.

Janet was experiencing the satisfaction of knowing that when her house-sitting task was behind her she would be moving into her own place. Her mind was full of dusting and cleaning and the necessity of buying furniture. But constantly intruding into her thoughts was the feeling of loss. She could not continue to see Adam unless it was on a personal basis. She refused to allow herself that dangerous luxury. She glanced over at him as he manoeuvred the car with the nonchalance of an expert driver and steeled herself to tell him how she felt. Not wanting the conversation to get maudlin, she tried to put a bright note in her voice.

'Well, it looks as if both our problems are solved,' she said. 'You're on your road to rehabiliation and I have my apartment.'

'And?' Adam prompted. His tight look warned her he had picked up the note of finality in her voice.

'We've had a very interesting week,' she said, 'and we've accomplished a lot. Now, I think——' The words came out round a lump in her throat and she repeated them. 'Now I think it's time for us to go our separate ways.'

'I knew you'd be coming to that,' said Adam, 'but we have one problem we haven't solved.'

'What's that?' Janet asked.

'Your rehabilitation. Don't you realise you carried a concealed weapon across country and broke a federal law? Now *I* have to rehabilitate *you*.'

'That's ridiculous!'

'Is it? Either you accept your rehabilitation or I turn you in. That's what you told me.'

'That's blackmail!' Janet expostulated, unbelieving.

'And who taught me?' said Adam. 'Take your choice—it's me or the police.'

CHAPTER SEVEN

'MISS TALBOT, would you like a cup of coffee?'

'Oh—yes, thank you,' Janet replied to Marsha Crookshank's question as she stood in the hall of Venitia House and realised that she'd probably been standing for some minutes like a robot whose batteries had run down.

The thin young woman with the wispy blonde hair hanging over her eyes watched Janet uneasily as if expecting the new counsellor to take some offence. The attitudes of the parolees seemed to fall into several categories. Marsha fell into that grouping of being over-eager to please and terrified of making any mistake that might send her back to prison.

Janet frowned at her retreating back, thinking Marsha would be difficult to handle properly. In her eagerness to make good she was likely to jump at the first opportunity that presented itself, and later be discouraged when she found she had chosen the wrong job. She'd need some careful guidance, but she wasn't Janet's client and Janet wasn't sure she was in a position to counsel anyone at that moment.

Janet's own life was in such a mess that it was taking all her attention, and that was why she'd been standing in the hall in a near-stupor. After Adam had taken her home on Saturday afternoon, he had left her at the kerb in front of the house and driven away with his threat of blackmail still ringing in her ears. She had argued with herself that he wouldn't make good his threat. Half afraid he might, she had spent most of the afternoon staring at the telephone, waiting for him to call, and rehearsing a variety of speeches guaranteed to slice him down to size.

By Sunday morning she had decided on a disdainful approach, daring him to report her. If he went to the police with his information, they'd certainly ask him how he knew about the gun, and he'd have to admit to his attempted burglary of the house. He couldn't possibly rat on her. By then her rehearsed speeches rang in her own ears with brilliance. But the telephone remained silent.

By Sunday afternoon she had decided what she had to do. She had to know the truth, and the best way to find out would be to go to the authorities.

How did a lawbreaker stand it? she wondered.

Afraid her fears would talk her out of her decision, she refused to allow herself to think as she put the gun in a paper bag and drove to the police station. When she arrived it seemed to be business as usual, though it was Sunday afternoon. She stood waiting for the desk sergeant to finish with a tearful woman who was sure her poodle had been stolen by a ring of dog thieves or her chief rival at the local dog show—the woman couldn't seem to make up her mind.

Janet stood as still as she kept her mind. She wouldn't allow herself to think. Her heart was beating in great painful thumps. Any moment, she thought, it must break her ribs. If this was the result of crime, why did anyone ever commit one?

'Yes, miss?'

The dog lady moved away and the cop was looking at her. She wanted to run, but she couldn't. Unable to stand the misery of inaction, she hurriedly stepped forward and placed the paper bag on the counter. 'I'd like to speak to someone concerning this gun,' she announced.

The sergeant peered into the bag, back at Janet and

over her shoulder at the group of people just entering and heading in his direction. 'Mike,' he called, 'would you take care of Miss——'

'Talbot,' said Janet, wishing she could have given an assumed name.

A younger officer, sitting at a desk behind the rail, rose and strode over to pick up the bag the sergeant indicated by a wave of his hand. The tag on the officer's shirt said 'Smith'. Janet wondered if he used an alias.

Back at his desk, he reached into the bag and took out the gun. After glancing at it, he laid it on the desk and indicated that Janet should take the chair facing him. 'What's the trouble?' he asked her.

'Well—er—tell me, how much trouble is a person in who transports a weapon across state lines?'

'It's a felony if it's transported for use in a crime. A felony under federal statute, that's over and above the fact of the criminal act itself.' His eyes twinkled. His easy manner surprised Janet, especially when eyebrows went up. 'Have you been committing a felony, Miss Talbot?'

His gentleness and humour caused her to relax slightly. 'Not deliberately, and would you mind if I pleaded the Fifth Amendment until I can clear my own mind slightly? Er—you see, I didn't intentionally bring it—I didn't even know I had it until I arrived in San Diego,' she paused, afraid of implicating her mother.

'Dad made sure you'd have protection?'

'No, it wasn't my father,' Janet answered with the relief of being able to speak honestly.

'Your mother.'

'Er—I don't remember.'

Officer Smith grinned.

She'd been trapped and didn't care for it. 'You figured things out rather quickly,' she said.

He laughed. 'I saw you as you came in. You were

scared to death, and holding the bag as if you were carrying a rattlesnake. The truth is, Mama wanted you to have some protection. Did the gun belong to her or to Dad?'

'My dad. He's an ex-policeman. *He* would have known better.'

'At the most, your crime is a misdemeanour.' He picked up the gun and removed the clip. 'Lot of good it would have done you. It's not even loaded.'

'I know,' Janet agreed. 'I wouldn't want to shoot it— am I in trouble?'

The officer sighed. 'Legally you shouldn't have done it, but there's the consideration of intent. You'll either have to register it or return it by legal means.'

Janet was so relieved that she felt as if her body was dissolving like melting ice cream.

'That's a tremendous relief! My friend said I'd be in considerable trouble, that it was a felony.'

Officer Smith grinned as he slid the weapon back in the bag. 'Your friend was either misinformed or pulling your leg.'

As she thought of Adam and his smug remarks, her eyes narrowed. She'd fix him!

'I doubt if it was ignorance of the law,' she snapped, her anger directed entirely towards Adam.

'Whoever it was——' Officer Smith paused, watching her intently. 'It was a *he*?'

'He!' grated Janet. 'Where can I get some bullets?' Then she smiled. 'Maybe I shouldn't have said that.'

'I wouldn't shoot him, Miss Talbot. I'd find some legal way to get back at him.'

'I'll do that,' she answered.

She remained in the chair for another twenty minutes while Officer Smith filled out a long report and explained to her how she could legally send the weapon back to her father. Or, if she chose to keep it, get it registered.

She returned to Harry Binns' house and put the gun in her suitcase until she could make arrangements for its legal shipment back to Iowa. Then she poured herself a glass of milk and sat down in the breakfast nook, wondering how she would get even with Adam Richfield. She was relieved to have the matter of the gun cleared up, but he deserved to have both ears cut off for scaring her so badly.

Adam would have been surprised to know Janet was thinking about him at all. On Monday morning he arrived early at the office. He talked with his survey party chiefs and then stood by listening while Rhoda pointed out a line of elevations she wanted run for an underground power line. Then, each carrying a cup of coffee, they went into Adam's office.

'How did your date go on Saturday?' Rhoda asked as soon as the door was closed.

'What are you doing? Vicariously living my love life?' Adam demanded.

'What else?' Rhoda sipped her coffee unconcerned. 'I'm a respectable married woman whose husband is out of town. You're better than television.'

'Well, I won't be from now on. She's decided we should go our separate ways.'

'And you don't want that.'

'I'm glad you told me what I want.'

'You didn't tell her the truth.'

'I tried. She's good at blocking the best intentions.'

'If you really wanted to, you could have blurted it out. She couldn't have stopped you.'

'That would have been smart. Then she'd think I deliberately made a fool of her.'

'You'd have been no worse off than you are now?'

'Six of one——'

The staccato sound of fingers drumming on the door interrupted Adam. The door opened and Norman looked in. Adam waved him forward.

'Another week, another dollar. What's up with you two?'

Rhoda gave Norman an accurate if short synopsis of Adam's love life as if the architect had every right to know. Adam threatened her life and her job and ordered her out of his office, but she ignored him.

'And he wants to keep on seeing her?' asked Norman.

'That's none of your business,' Adam told him.

'He does,' Rhoda said.

'If you were a woman, what would change *your* mind?' Norman asked Rhoda.

Adam gave a bark of laughter, but Rhoda didn't think it was funny.

'If I were a woman?'

While Adam laughed, Rhoda glowered at Norman, who sat perplexed, knowing he'd committed a solecism but not how to correct it.

'You always prided yourself on being one of the guys,' Adam teased her.

'That's carrying the buddy system too far,' snapped Rhoda.

'Wait a minute—I'll rephrase that,' Norman said hesitantly. 'If you were Janet Talbot?'

Rhoda wasn't completely mollified, but she returned to the subject at hand.

'*I* think he should play on her sympathies,' she said immediately.

'You're out of your mind!' Adam swung his chair so that his back was to them.

'She's into rehabilitation,' Rhoda continued. 'He should tell her he's going back into a life of crime.'

'And then she'll start rehabilitating him again?'

Norman asked.

'Right.'

'Wrong!' Adam swung back to face them. 'She'd have me locked up.'

Janet was aware she had wasted part of her morning, and after Marsha Crookshank had brought her the coffee she returned to the office, determined to put Adam out of her mind and make up for her lapse. Pete Hall, the house director and her boss, came through the door jingling his car keys.

'I'll run an errand and meet you at the unemployment office,' he said.

Janet glanced down at her watch, once more guiltily realising she'd let far too much of the morning get away from her while she thought about Adam. Pete was including her in a preliminary meeting with some local state officials. They were to discuss the ways and means of implementing some changes in the Local Vocational Investigative Programme. Janet knew she should be sensible of the opportunity and push her personal problems to the back of her mind.

'Yes, I'll follow along in a few minutes,' she said.

'Remember how to get there?' he asked, heading for the front entrance.

'I think I can make it,' Janet called with forced gaiety.

And true to her word, she did locate the unemployment office again. Because of the parking problem she had to park almost three blocks away, and on a side street round the corner from Associated Architects and Engineers.

As she turned the corner and started up the street, she appraised the building with the casual curiosity of indirectly knowing one of the partners of the engineering company. Then the main door of the building opened and two men stepped outside and walked slowly down the sidewalk. They were in deep conversation, and Janet recognised the tall, lithe frame of Adam Richfield. His collar was casually open, his shirt sleeves rolled up to the elbows as if he'd been working, and he appeared relaxed and confident. The other man was dressed in khaki, wore heavy work boots, and had a large roll of drawings under his arm. They parted amicably, shaking hands. Adam turned and strolled back up the sidewalk, and the stranger crossed the street and climbed into a pick-up truck.

Janet, not wanting to be recognised, had stood close to a shrubbery and was still watching when Adam disappeared back inside the building.

'Excuse me,' said a masculine voice behind her.

She jumped, and turned to see the smiling face of a mailman who pushed a three-wheeled cart. 'Oh, pardon me,' she said. She stepped out of his way and then thought better of her move. 'May I ask you a question?'

The postman paused with an amiable expression as he waited.

Janet pointed to the engineering company. 'What businesses are in that building? Could you tell me?'

'Just the engineering company,' he said. 'Used to be broken up into offices, but Richfield bought the building, and as the tenants moved out he took it over completely.'

Janet stared at him. 'Richfield?'

'Yeah, he's the senior partner. Other one's name is—Barnes? Burns——'

'Binns?' Janet suggested.

'Binns,' the postman sounded positive after her reminder. 'Must do okay; it's a good-sized building. If you're looking for one of the lawyers that used to be in there, check over in that new office building. They're not on my route, so I can't help much.'

'Thank you,' said Janet, and walked on down the street, content to let the postman think she was looking for a legal firm.

The direction she travelled was her route to the unemployment office, and her heels pounded the pavement as she seethed. Richfield and Binns, Richfield and Binns was the chant of her outrage that kept time with her striding.

At the meeting, her lack of input was taken as the shyness of a new person on a job. Later that afternoon she could barely remember two words of the serious and involved discussion. Nor did she accomplish much the rest of the day.

When she arrived back at Harry Binns' house that evening, she threw her handbag down on the hall table and strode up and down the hall, needing its length to work out her frustrations.

Adam Richfield was Harry Binns' *partner*! *Senior partner*!

Why hadn't he told her? He'd made a fool of her. At least, he'd deliberately allowed her to make a fool of herself.

Logic and honesty tried to intrude, pointing out that she'd given him no chance to explain himself. Her anger argued back. He could have insisted. She couldn't have stopped him if he had demanded she should listen. She was holding a gun on him. She didn't know how to shoot it. He didn't know that. She hadn't been holding a gun on him on Wednesday, Friday or Saturday!

Harry Binns' partner! She marched into the den, intending to go to the kitchen and slam a few cabinet doors in the process of fixing a light meal. Then out of the corner of her eye she chanced to notice the drafting table and desk again. A thought brought her up short.

She remembered the telephone call from a Norman somebody. Until then she'd forgotten about her delivery of the file folder. She'd taken him the papers she'd removed from the drafting table when she cleaned it off that Monday evening. What had happened to the drawings and prints she had so carefully rolled and labelled? She marched over to the big round painted bin that held the stored rolls. A careful inspection told her the bundle she'd made was no longer in that bin.

So that was why he'd been in the house. He'd got in to get a roll of drawings, and because she had put the file folder in the desk he hadn't found it. Norman whosit had called because they knew she was staying in the house and they couldn't risk another break-in.

Her assessment of the situation seemed accurate enough, but Janet felt it lacked the solidity of proof. She stared at the desk and then at the closet door close by.

In an earlier search for a place to store her empty luggage, she'd discovered a closet and two filing cabinets within it. Not one to pry into other people's business, it hadn't occurred to her even to read the labels on the outside of the drawers. But the need of proof overrode her natural disinclination to pry. She jerked the door open and looked down at the filing cabinet drawers. No need to read the labels—they were blank.

She tested the first drawer. It slid open at a touch. Apparently Harry Binns felt no need to lock up records in his own house. She looked down at the tattered manila file folders. Each was well used and labelled, with names that meant nothing to Janet. She pulled out one and saw that it contained folded blueprints and pages of neat, closely written computations.

In the third drawer down she spotted a folder whose legend read, 'Advertisement', and in her haste to pull it out she brought another file with it, spilling the contents of the second file on the floor.

She gathered up the scraps of odd-looking sheets of

lines, squares and dots, and several pages of rub-on letters. Sitting on the floor by the cabinet, she opened the folder on advertisement, and after several pages of notes and mock-ups she found a paste-up of a flyer, announcing the opening of the firm. Her attention riveted on the two photographs near the top of the page. One was of a smiling, round-faced man with twinkling eyes. He was vaguely familiar. She wasn't surprised; she and Harry had grown up in neighbouring counties back in Iowa. The other photograph bore the rugged features of Adam Richfield, a few years younger, but unmistakable.

Proof enough, Janet thought, and gathering up the two folders she put them back in the cabinet and slammed the drawer closed with a vengeance.

In the kitchen she opened the refrigerator and reached for a carton of milk, but changed her mind. Milk was soothing to the nerves, and she wanted full mileage out of her anger. She chose instead to make a pot of coffee. And while the automatic pot dripped and gurgled, she mentally blasted Adam Richfield with words that had never crossed her lips. He'd made a fool of her, and she wasn't going to let him get away with it. He'd allowed her to think he was a criminal! Well, that's been your problem, the logic of her mind insisted. You didn't want him to be a criminal. Be happy he's not.

'Oh, shut up!' Janet vocalised her feelings against that unemotional part of her which tried to maintain at least a semblance of sanity.

He'd tried to make a fool of her by saying he was going to start an escort service. He had even talked about advertising. Suddenly her mind was still. Advertising . . .

Janet returned to the closet, opened the third door of the filing cabinet and removed the two folders, the one with the mock-up and the one with the graphic supplies. She carried them to the desk, and with a silent apology to Harry Binns, searched through his desk for several sheets of plain bond paper.

Her high school experience in helping lay out the school paper was rusty, but she didn't need to be perfect.

By the time the coffee pot had finished gurgling, she'd made two trial sketches and knew what she wanted to do. Back in the kitchen she poured the coffee, added a considerable amount of sugar because she felt she needed the energy, and returned to the desk.

Adam Richfield was in for a surprise!

She needed his home telephone number. Her searching gaze spotted Harry's personal telephone directory, and she found the number listed on the first line of the page under 'R.'

Janet picked up the phone and dialled, her heart beating wildly. She'd hang up if he answered. She couldn't let him know it was her. The thought of doing something so rude and childish caused her face to warm and her blood to pound, but this was war!

The voice that came over the phone after the third ring was definitely his, but it held the lack of personal warmth particular to a recording.

This is Adam Richfield. I'm not in right now . . .

She hung up the phone. She had all she needed to get even with him.

On Wednesday evening Adam pushed the button on his television remote, turning off the set. He wasn't impressed with the day's news. Nothing held his attention for long.

When he'd come in that evening he'd fixed a Scotch and water. But after his third sip he pushed it across to the extreme edge of the end table by his easy chair. A stupid, churlish move, he thought. Just part of his irritation at life in general and Janet Talbot in particular. He'd never thought of himself as a ladykiller, but he'd dodged his share of predatory females. And more often dodged than pursued. Janet Talbot had wounded his pride—twice—and while he'd put on a face of bravado and threatened to blackmail her, he wasn't sure his ploy had worked. He was a little afraid to put it to the test.

'Hell, the world's full of women. I don't need her.' He spoke to the blank eye of the television and then stretched across the table to pull the drink back towards him.

His hand, reaching across to the telephone, paused and picked up the receiver, and he stared at it a moment before dropping it back in its cradle. Why should he call to be told she didn't want to see him? If she'd changed her mind she could call *him*. He was listed in the directory. His number was probably plastered all over Harry's house! But she wouldn't know that.

She could look in the telephone directory.

As he lifted the drink, the telephone rang. He picked up the receiver before the answering machine could engage.

'Adam Richfield!' His voice was so sharp he'd scare his caller to death.

'Adam Richfield of the Personal Escort Service?' The voice was female, soft, whispery with nervousness, but he caught a hint of the mid-Western accent, and something else he couldn't quite identify.

The mid-Western flavour could only be Janet, he decided, and the quality he couldn't quite catch could come from her efforts to disguise her voice. He was right, he thought. By waiting her out, he'd forced her to do the calling.

'Correct. Escort at your service, ma'am,' he answered, his smile widening until he wondered if it travelled over the phone.

'Well—er—Mr Richfield, I'm a stranger in town and—er—I wondered if you were by any chance free this evening?'

'As I said, at your service.' Adam's voice had turned slightly seductive. Janet was playing a good game, but if she wanted to smooth over the situation he wouldn't put any stumbling blocks in her way.

'My name is Addie Martin and I'm staying at the Westgate Hotel. I'd like to see some of the nightlife of San Diego,' his caller continued, still sounding a little frightened and hesitant.

'I'd be glad to show it to you,' Adam said, offering her all the encouragement he felt. 'Would you like to meet me in the lobby? Say, in about an hour?'

'Oh, that would be just fine.'

'See you in an hour,' said Adam. Hanging up the phone, he gulped down the rest of the drink and carried the glass to the kitchen, putting it in the sink and nearly breaking it in his haste.

So Janet wanted to play games. He didn't mind at all.

He hurried to the bathroom and turned on the shower with one hand while he unbuttoned his shirt with the other. He whistled as he stepped in the shower. An hour later he strode into the Westgate Hotel, slowing his steps as he looked around.

A blonde standing by a plant across the lobby caught his attention, but as she turned he saw it wasn't Janet. He looked at his watch. He was five minutes early. Maybe he'd just take a chair and wait until she showed up.

'Mr Richfield?'

Adam turned to see an elderly woman approaching him, peering at him with timid birdlike eyes and comparing him with a blue leaflet in her hand. His surprise held him still and silent.

She consulted the leaflet again and then looked back at him. 'You *are* Mr Richfield, aren't you? You look a little older than your picture. I'm Addie Martin.' Now he recognised the voice quality he hadn't caught over the phone. He'd mistaken the tremulous waver of age for a disguise.

'Er—yes, I'm Adam Richfield.' Confused to the point of stupidity, he reached out a hand and gently lifted the blue pamphlet from her unresisting fingers. Emblazoned across the top were three words in heavy black letters.

RICHFIELD ESCORT SERVICE

Below was a picture of himself. He recognised the photograph and knew its origin immediately. It had been used on the advertisement flyer when he and Harry had opened the business. Below the picture was a list of activities and services offered by the escort service. His anger turned cold. He was going to *murder* Janet Talbot!

'Mr Richfield, is anything wrong?'

'Er—no. No,' Adam snapped. When he noticed the anxiety on the little woman's face, he smiled. 'No, I was just thinking I need to have another picture made. Such an inconvenience,' he said, tucking the pamphlet in his pocket.

He stood for a moment, irresolute. He'd fix Janet Talbot, but at the moment what was he going to do with Addie Martin? She'd picked up the pamphlet in good faith. She was watching him a little doubtfully, and was pulling away his normal reserve towards strangers by forcibly reminding him of his grandmother. She looked about seventy; there was a certain homespun quality about her, but along with her nervousness he saw an indomitable spirit in her faded blue eyes. Despite her age, she was like a child on holiday. The tinge of mischief in her expression, her hesitant trust in him, brought out a feeling of begrudged responsibility. Around his anger came the tendrils of sympathy and genuine liking for this little woman. He knew he couldn't disappoint her.

'So tell me, Miss Martin,' he said, attempting to keep his voice light and carefree, 'what is your pleasure for the evening?'

Her pale eyes, surrounded by the wrinkles of age, suddenly became worried.

'I don't really know,' she turned shy, twisting a pair of white gloves. Adam stared at them and wondered how long it was since he's seen a women wear white gloves.

'You see, I've lived all my life in a small town—and just once I'd like to see a nightclub or——' she looked up quickly, '—nothing risqué, understand—but when one's lived to be sixty-eight and never seen anything——'

Adam smiled down at her. He was right—she could have been his grandmother, who might have had the temerity to leave a small town in Arizona and travel to a big city. She might have made that telephone call, but like Addie Martin she would have stopped short of being risqué.

'Kansas,' he mused, and remembered Janet's mid-Western enthusiasm for the ocean. 'My dear Addie, why don't you sit down and let me call a restaurant I know of? I think I know the perfect place for dinner.'

While Addie Martin sat primly on a chair in the lobby, he went to the telephone booth nearby and, using the directory, looked up the number of the Marine Room, where the diners sat almost at beach level and watched the waves roll towards them on the shore. After he'd made his reservation, he was walking past a rack of fliers advertising various activities in the city when he spotted the blue folders.

After he'd strangled Janet Talbot, he was going to shoot her, stab her, and boil her in oil!

He grabbed the dozen or so folders and shoved them in his pocket. But by the time he returned to the little lady from Kansas, he'd smothered the anger from his face and showed her an encouraging smile.

On Thursday morning the surveyors had left when Adam strode up the hall. He was later than usual, tardy because of a lack of sleep. His eyelids felt as though their inner layers had been sandpapered. But he'd given little Miss Addie Martin an evening to remember for the rest of her life. He'd done too good a job, he reflected. Addie still had two days left of her vacation in San Diego and had engaged his services for both evenings. He'd enjoyed the little lady's excitement, though he was sure he'd be bored before she was on the plane returning to Kansas. Part of his problem would be how to keep her from paying him. He had no doubt she was using some carefully hoarded savings for her small adventure.

After he'd left her at the elevator in the Westgate, he'd visited five other hotels. In each one, he'd picked up between seven and a dozen blue pamphlets. Not knowing how many Janet had distributed had kept him awake the rest of the night

Now, as he strode up the hall, he paused long enough to open the door into the engineering department and shout, 'Rhoda! Come up to my office! Now!'

He'd just entered and slammed the door when Rhoda opened it and came in, quieter than usual.

He strode over to the cupboard and grabbed the yellow pages of the telephone directory, impatiently pushing at the pages until he found the listing of hotels.

'Make a list of every hotel in this town,' he told her. He picked up a pen and made checkmarks beside the six hotels he'd visited.

'Skip these six, but go to the rest. Look on the racks of fliers of activities and pick up these damn things,' he said as he pulled one of the blue pamphlets from his pocket.

Rhoda had been standing in a position of defence as though she had expected to do battle for one of her people, or find herself fired. She allowed her jaw to drop as she picked up the blue mimeographed paper and stared at it. 'She didn't!' she exclaimed, her lips trembling.

Adam, still staring at the list of hotels, hadn't noticed her expression.

'You better believe she did—I can't go myself, I've got a meeting at the city——' He looked up to see his project engineer's face, a comic combination of awe and delight that Janet had caught him with a twist on his own trick. He felt as if he could rip the top off his desk.

'If you laugh you're fired,' he warned her, not totally convinced it was an empty threat.

'I know it.' Her voice was as unsteady as her lips, though it carried all the sincerity of firm belief. 'So I'd better get out of here.' She grabbed the telephone directory and rushed from the room.

'Damn that woman! She's back in her office laughing her head off!' He glowered at the door then reached for his personal telephone directory. He'd let Janet Talbot know what he thought of her scheme!

But when he reached Venitia House, he learned she was not on duty. He called the Binns' place, but after ten rings he hung up. Either she chose not to answer or she was out. Probably out, he decided. She'd talked about needing to buy furniture. After several abortive attempts he scribbled a hasty note to Rhoda, and left the building. When his meeting was over he was picking up Addie Martin. He had promised to take her to Sea

World. Despite his mood, he smiled as he thought of the little woman waiting anxiously to see the sights of San Diego. Since the marine amusement park stayed open in the evenings, she'd probably enjoy it, and it was certainly innocuous.

Of course, with his luck, he'd probably be spat on by the walrus.

Janet had spent a busy Tuesday evening folding more than a hundred of the five hundred blue photocopies she'd had made.

'Why so many?' she asked herself when she picked them up, but knew the answer. When she'd placed the order that morning, she'd been angry enough to paper the world with pamphlets about Adam Richfield.

Part of her anger had been soothed by Tuesday evening, but not enough to prevent her from going on with her scheme. Using her map and the telephone directory from Harry Binns' house, she learned quite a bit about San Diego as she drove from hotel to hotel. She had pretended to look at the activities of fliers on the rack, and had inserted a few of the blue pamphlets among the other advertisements before moving on to the next hotel. By the time she'd been to a dozen different lobbies, the evening had progressed into night and she returned to the Binns' house. She went to sleep visualising Adam Richfield's anger when he discovered what she'd done.

By Wednesday evening at six-thirty, she couldn't stand the suspense any longer. She dialled his number and got a busy signal. She knew she was jumping to conclusions by deciding the call he was in the process of taking was from a prospective client, but she sat at Harry's desk and hugged herself, not willing to admit it could be anything else.

Any moment, she thought, he'd call. He was going to

be mad, but she wasn't worried about that. The madder he was, the better she'd like it! If he wasn't enraged, she'd failed.

At seven she was still waiting.

At seven-thirty she decided to make sure the front door was locked. If he wasn't calling, he'd certainly come over.

At ten-thirty she slammed every cabinet door in the kitchen. In the bedroom she kicked her shoes under the bed before she turned of the light.

She didn't sleep well on Wednesday night. Her rest was interrupted by dreams of Adam escorting beautiful women around town. She could barely close her eyes before he'd stroll across her inner vision with some ravishing charmer on his arm.

She was up at dawn, weighted down by depression. If he found some gorgeous delightful creature, she'd be the one responsible. After all, she'd put out those pamphlets. She argued with herself, insisting she couldn't care less. Possibly she should feel some concern for the poor woman who would sooner or later form a permanent relationship with Adam. His pranks were guaranteed to destroy her peace of mind if not her sanity.

She wasn't sheduled to work that Thursday, so after several cups of strong coffee she dressed in her oldest clothes and checked the supplies in the back of her car before locking the Binns' house. A broom, dustpan, soap, window cleaner, paper towels, mop, wastebasket, etcetera. If she'd forgotten anything, she'd find a market close to her new apartment or do without. Cleaning her new place would be just the therapy she needed. A touch of South Pacific, she reflected. She was going to scrub him out of her life. Washing windows and scrubbing floors were less glamorous than washing hair, but all that mattered was that she should rid herself of Adam Richfield.

But the scrubbing and the scouring didn't take him out of her mind. As she cleaned the inside of already clean cabinets, and washed the disuse from the kitchen counters, sink and bathroom fixtures, she rehashed all her grievances and rehearsed more brilliantly scathing speeches. She resolutely fought the logical objections that insisted upon trying to undermine her sense of ill-use.

Okay, her primary reason for wanting Adam Richfield out of her life had been his criminal background and her fear that he'd end up in jail as Derek had. So what? She would have been delighted to learn he was a law-abiding citizen if *he* had told her. But *he* didn't. Why should that make such a difference? logic cried. Shut up! Mind your own business!

He hadn't told her. He'd let her fall in love with him, complicated her life, compromised her sense of morals and duty, and done it all with a trick. She couldn't be sure whether the blur she was seeing was caused by tears or window cleaner. Window cleaner, she decided. She *refused* to cry over Adam Richfield.

CHAPTER EIGHT

'YOU *have* to do something.' Rhoda set her coffee cup down on the edge of Adam's desk.

He stared at the slanting shaft of early Monday sunlight. It fell on a series of circles, made by the coffee cups placed on the outer edge of the desk. They had become more numerous as Adam, Rhoda and Norman picked up and put down their cups. They were having another of what had become customary early morning meetings. As usual of late, the discussion centred on Adam's problem with Janet Talbot. As he eyed the marks, he thought of the circles in his life since he'd met that woman.

'Well, what can he do?' asked Norman. 'And why should he do anything? She knows the truth now. He's well out of it.'

'Norman's right,' Adam said, drawing circles on a yellow pad. 'I've spent too much time on that stupid broad.'

'If she was stupid, you wouldn't have bothered,' Rhoda countered. 'And don't tell me you'll let it drop.'

'He should. Much more of her, and when Harry comes back there won't be a business,' muttered Norman.

'I can handle my personal life and the company,' Adam snapped.

Norman stopped his complaints and Rhoda looked triumphant.

Adam thought of the circles again. The arguments were having the opposite effect of their intent. Rhoda, pushing for a romance, was driving him to reject Janet.

145

Norman, wanting life normal again, was pushing him into it. And their ability to influence him warned Adam that his own state of mind was none too stable, at least where Janet was concerned.

He'd always made his own decisions. Rhoda had been his confidante for years and knew a lot about his life, but he'd never allowed her to run it. Maybe Norman was right. Maybe he shouldn't try to see Janet again. She'd certainly been a disturbing influence.

'. . . it would work,' Rhoda was saying. 'If she thought he was going back to his criminal ways, she'd start rehabilitating him all over again.'

'Rhoda, get off that kick,' Adam demanded. 'She knows I'm not a burglar. She knows who I am.'

'Want me to talk to her?'

'Hell, no! I'll do my own talking.' Once he'd made the statement, he knew he'd made the right decision—the only decision for him. When he'd do it, he wasn't sure. Life, he thought, was one hell of a mess.

Janet was despondent when she arrived home on Monday evening. Over the weekend her knowledge of the world had been widened considerably. She'd never suspected there were so many brands of mattress sets, nor that they could vary so widely in construction, materials, prices and guarantees.

She'd spent Sunday afternoon strolling through the furniture stores, growing more and more bewildered. On Monday she decided she was right to work on priorities. Her necessities, in order to move into the apartment, would include a box spring and mattress on which to sleep and a breakfast set so that she had a place to eat. The rest of her furniture could be bought as she found what she wanted. Her dishes, kitchen utensils and linens were being shipped by her parents. Most of the items were farewell gifts from family and friends back in Iowa who took a vicarious thrill in seeing her start her own life. In her bleak mood, she was wondering how many of those gifts would be consigned to the upper shelves of the kitchen and linen closets when she formed her own style of décor.

When she unlocked the front door of the Binns' house, she immediately noticed the odour.

Food.

Had she left something on the stove that morning? She had a vision of ruined pots and a charred stove surface in her mind as she slammed the door and dropped her handbag and keys on the hall table, hurrying to the kitchen.

There were pots on the burners. She hadn't put them there. In the sink were several paper cartons, white boxes with wire handles, the kind used by Oriental restaurants for take-out orders. On the counter stood a bottle of rice wine. Harry Binns had cut short his vacation and returned, she decided. While she stood looking at the food, her mind immediately made an inventory of the house, wondering what she might have left lying about. She'd been careful to keep it neat, but when she was in a hurry she scattered things about until she resembled a tree shedding leaves.

'Mister Binns?' she called softly. 'Harry?'

'Sorry, he's still in Canada,' came an answer from the den.

Her heart gave a flip as she recognised Adam's voice.

'This is the answering service,' he continued in a monotone, like a computerised voice.

Janet walked into the den where he sat on the playpen, leaning against the back of the sofa cushion at the edge of the unit. His feet were stretched out on an ottoman as he read the evening paper.

'How did you get in?' she demanded, not knowing what else to say. Her emotions were warring over her delight at seeing him and his high-handedness at not giving her the right of refusal.

'My usual way,' Adam jerked his head in the direction of the window he'd used the week before.

'When your partner returns,' Janet answered. 'I'm going to suggest he should board up that window.'

'Oh, he doesn't have to worry. I never climb in to see him.'

'I can't help wondering why you climbed in to see me,' she said, all her outrage returning again as she thought of how he had tricked her. She ignored her heart, which seemed to be skipping around like a happy puppy.

'I decided we needed to straighten out our misunderstandings,' Adam answered calmly.

'As far as I can tell, we're straight. You tried to make a fool out of me and you succeeded. Congratulations.'

'I can understand your feelings,' he began, still keeping his eye on the newspaper.

Janet, standing just beyond the doorway of the kitchen, felt foolish and awkward and wasn't sure whether to retreat, advance or remain implacably where she was.

'I know how I'd feel if someone made a game of me.' He folded the paper and lifted his long legs, turning slightly to lower his feet to the floor. Then he stood and strolled towards her. Not sure what he intended, she stepped aside and he continued on into the kitchen. He seemed perfectly at home as he took the dishes from the cupboards and placed them on the corner near the breakfast table.

'Of course, it doesn't make you feel any better to know when I went along with your sceheme that I did it because you'd scared the hell out of *me*.'

Janet edged into the kitchen and stood watching him. 'I wouldn't think you scared easily,' she said. The hesitancy in her voice irritated her, but she couldn't be sure he wasn't telling the truth.

'Not physically,' Adam answered as he opened a drawer and took out two place mats for the table. 'I didn't really think you'd shoot me.' He walked on into the the breakfast nook and started arranging the table. 'But consider what would happen to the company if I were accused of criminal acts. I had to think of Harry as well as myself, *and* our employees.'

'Oh.' Janet suddenly saw the situation in a different light.

'I mean, I'm senior partner. How would it look to our clients?' He was busy putting the knives on the wrong side of the plates.

Janet felt as if she was watching a play. The entire scene was unreal. He was confusing her.

'But I think——' she started to object, when he cut her off.

'You think I should have told you. But the question is when. Remember, I couldn't prove I was getting a set of plans when I broke in that night. That's really what I was doing.'

'I figured that out,' she said.

'Yeah, but look at my position. Norman had taken the plans from me through the window,' said Adam. 'He'd gone.'

'And you were going through the house,' Janet murmured. She was questioning his act, but then she saw the answer herself. 'You'd fastened the window from the inside and the front door would lock behind you.'

Adam nodded and returned to the kitchen, where he switched off the heat under the pots.

'But you could have told me,' she fell back on her major objection, the one she'd been clinging to for a week. It had been the raft of injustice that her kept her afloat throughout those seven miserable days; she was afraid to let go.

'When?' He took two bowls from the cupboard, filling one with steaming white rice and the other with sweet and sour pork. 'When were you ready to hear the truth? What was the exact moment when you would have believed me *and* when you would have forgiven the trick?'

He turned, handling her the bowl of rice, and she took it automatically, staring down into the mound of steaming white grains as if they held the answer.

'I don't know,' she admitted honestly.

'Well, neither did I.'

Janet carried the bowl to the table, put it carefully on the hot mat he'd placed and then asked herself, what was she doing? She was allowing him to calmly talk away her outrage. And she wasn't ready to let go her resentment.'

'Now, wait a minute. This isn't fair,' she insisted. 'You made a fool of me, but the way you're telling it, it's all *my* fault!'

When Adam tried to hand her a bowl of Chinese noodles she stepped aside, her hands behind her back. Seeing her unwillingness to help he shrugged and lined the rest of the food and the saké up on the counter that separated the kitchen and the breakfast nook. Then he stepped round the barrier to transfer the rest of the dinner to the table.

'And you seem very familiar with Harry's house,' she accused him.

'Naturally. We started our company in the den—pre-playpen days.' He opened the wine and poured it into two saké cups. 'And you're wrong. The fault wasn't yours.' He held a chair for her, but she refused to sit. He left the chair out and took his place across the table.

As he dished out the noodles, rice and sweet and sour

pork, Janet's mouth watered. But she resisted the temptation. She wasn't letting him win her over so easily. If he wanted her to forgive and forget, he'd have to do better than he'd done so far.

'You behaved exactly as you should have,' he glanced up at her. 'You shouldn't miss this. I think Lu Wong makes the best Chinese food in the country.'

'I was just wondering if I'd invited you to dinner,' Janet hedged.

'Of course you did.' Adam started filling her plate. 'You see the reason for clearing up the problem as well as I do.'

She didn't, and when he looked up he could tell by her expression.

'You're from Harry's part of the country, your families know each other, and he'll be keeping in touch with you. He'll probably invite you to his parties. We'll meet from time to time.'

'I suppose so,' Janet said flatly, suddenly deciding to sit. Her knees felt weak, and the pain in her chest was preventing her from breathing properly. He wasn't trying to cajole her into a good mood. He was straightening out all the misunderstandings before he said goodbye to her. The thought of never seeing him again was paralysing. She'd been telling herself for the last week that he was permanently out of her life, but she hadn't really believed it. She struggled to find something to counter it, tugging at pride to fill the sudden void.

'I don't regret making up those pamphlets,' she announced defensively. 'You deserved it.'

'Of course I did,' he agreed with unimpaired amiability. 'I congratulate you. That was a brilliant move.'

Janet eyed him with dissatisfaction as he continued his meal. She wasn't quite sure why she'd brought up the fliers. Perhaps as a test to see if she could arouse his anger—anything would have been better than his acceptance of everything that had happened. It seemed that with his mathematical mind he'd put all the incidents of the past two weeks into neat columns and had given each a total. Then he'd consigned the sum of the experience to a file, neatly marked, and tucked it away in one of his metal cabinets. But Janet didn't want to be put away in a file, neatly totalled. Probably with a greater sum in the liability column. Lu Wong's food might have been good, but her taste had atrophied along with the shrivelling of her hopes.

When Adam filled her saké cup again, she drank it down. The strong liquid was no more than water against her paralysed senses.

'You think I tricked *you*,' said Adam, and from the emotion in his voice he could have been retelling a tale he'd overheard. 'When we strolled into the Bali Hai and I spotted one of my regular contractors, I knew I'd outdone myself.'

'Then he wasn't a cop?' Janet asked, willing to let the conversation drift rather than allow her mind to escape into other channels.

'No. And he would have blown my cover in a minute.'

'You do have a criminal mind,' she observed.

Adam seemed doubtful. 'Rather a highly developed sense of self-preservation,' he said.

After telling her about the contractor, Adam gave his attention to the food. Janet, still feeling as if the floor had slipped from beneath her feet, was as confused as ever. Her pride refused to allow him to see her misery and she tried to force herself to eat, to act as if it meant nothing to her that he had merely wanted to straighten out the trouble before he walked out of her life.

She attempted to marshal her thoughts, wanting to make light conversation to show him that he mattered no more to her than any other casual acquaintance. But her heart refused to allow her brain to function properly. Her clever remarks were dammed up behind a boulder of pain. It throbbed, he's leaving, he's leaving, he's leaving.

Adam raised his head and gave her a slow lazy smile. 'I have a question.'

'Oh?' Banal, Janet thought, but she wasn't able to do any better.

'How did you find out?' He dropped his eyes to his plate. 'I know the picture came from Harry's files——'

'I didn't look in the files until I knew!' Janet was suddenly defensive again, Pride had won. 'I'm not a snoop!'

'You knew before you found the picture?'

'Have you forgotten the state unemployment office down the block from your building? We work closely with them. If you want to hide, don't walk your clients to their cars—or trucks.'

'Barnes.' The word was an accusation.

'That was the name on the side of the truck.'

'He's a pain sometimes. He keeps the most important reason for his visit until he's outside—then I have to follow him down the walk.' Adam smiled again. 'That proves it. I wouldn't make a good criminal. I'd get busy and walk straight into a cop.'

'Or your parole officer?'

'Right.'

Once they had exhausted the subject, they returned their attention to their plates.

Janet couldn't face another mouthful, nor, she decided, could she continue to sit at that table knowing it was only a matter of time before he left for good. Waiting for the inevitable was unbearable. She carefully placed her fork across her plate and removed the napkin from her lap, putting it beside the plate.

'Thank you for dinner,' she said, not looking at him. 'And thank you for the explanation.'

She rose and started stacking the dishes, needing something to occupy her hands. Hardly gracious, she thought, to begin clearing the table while he was still sitting. But her hands worked automatically.

He rose from his place and helped her. 'And thank you for *your* explanations,' he answered as he carried the plates into the kitchen.

'And thank you for helping me find the apartment,' Janet added, not to be outdone. How long could they continue these halting commonplaces? she wondered.

'Have you bought any furniture?' he asked.

Obviously they could go on for a while.

Janet, rinsing the dishes before putting them in the dishwasher, shook her head.

'It's not easy furnishing a place,' Adam said. 'I'd like to do something about mine. Haven't the faintest idea of how to start.'

'I don't know either,' Janet admitted. At the moment she couldn't think well enough to walk across the floor if her legs hadn't acted independently of her conscious thought. She was numb from the heart up. Her mind was caught up with the man beside her as he took the paper cartons from the sink, rinsed and crushed them before putting them in the bin.

'You know,' he said slowly, 'we're pretty good at helping each other——' He paused as she looked up at him wide-eyed. He'd lost some of that poise, he seemed hesistant, though insistent. 'No, stop and think about it. Even working at cross-purposes, we did each other some good. If we were honest, and started out to complete something together, we'd do a lot better.'

'I don't understand,' Janet said. She warned herself not to hope.

'I know the city,' he explained. 'I've some idea of

where the better furniture stores are. You must know more about decorating than I do——'

Unwilling to face him, Janet grabbed a sponge and energetically scrubbed the spotless counter. 'I thought you wanted to clear the air and say goodbye.'

Adam, who had returned to the breakfast nook, removed the place mats from the table. He seemed to be moving in slow motion. 'If we've cleared the air, what's the problem? Straight business deal. I do the driving, find the stores, and you give advice. A trade-off.'

Janet had warned herself not to hope. Why didn't she listen to herself?

'I think we've finished the kitchen,' Adam said as he put the place mats back in the drawer. 'Is it a deal?'

She kept her eyes fixed on the kitchen counter, determined not to look at him. He stood some distance away, his back to the counter, his hands resting lightly on the curves of the edge as he stood, one foot crossed slightly over the other.

Logic demanded she should say no. If he was walking out of her life, let him go. Pride, too, said send him on his way. Her voice followed the promptings of her heart and her traitorous emotions that clung to hope—hope that could only be a cruel illusion.

Twenty minutes later, Adam parked the car in the lot of a large furniture store and switched off the engine.

'Ultra-modern,' he said with shrug. 'I don't know that this is my style.'

'If it isn't, at least we'll know what we don't want.'

Adam raised his eyebrows, 'We?'

Janet's chin rose to match. 'We. I'm not sure I'm interested in ultra-modern either.'

Because of the construction in progress, the front of the building had been roped off and they entered by the side door. Denied the hints of window displays in the glass windows, they were struck by the full glory of modern curved pole lamps arching across the backs of sofas to droop over coffee tables. Bright plastic tables glared at white sofas. Huge white tulip lamps, made of lucite, gleamed from hidden bulbs.

When Janet's step faltered, Adam took her arm and led her forward. 'We're here, we might as well look,' he murmured. 'As you said, we'll learn what we don't want. I've learned something already.'

'Umm,' Janet murmured as she considered the white tulip lamp on a black lacquered cube table and wondered if green leaves would help it. She decided against the leaves. Nothing could save that monstrosity.

'Now I know where old bicylce handles go to die,' Adam explained, gazing at another lamp.

She surveyed the free-standing chrome pole on which chrome tubing twisted and bent to hold four clear glass globes. The centres of the glass balls were lit with candlebulbs. The electric arc of their illumination was stark and unshaded. But Janet thought Adam was too severe.

'Unkind,' she said. 'Someone will give that lamp a nice home.'

'You, possibly.'

'Possibly,' she retorted, with no intention of doing so, but she couldn't let him win with two words.

He didn't disagree. Instead he guided her to a large white leather chair in the arrangement and seated her as he took a place on the end of the sofa by the pole lamp. 'What type of furniture would you put with it?' he asked.

'I don't know,' Janet thought as she gazed at him, thinking how comfortable and at home he appeared on the sofa. She tried to imagine the entire setting in the carriage house she'd rented, but unaccountably those sharp points of light from the lamp seemed to be getting in the way of her imagination. She blinked and turned her head away. When she looked back she saw his infuriatingly superior smile.

'You win,' she said warily. 'With that creature, you'd have to wear sunglasses in the living-room.'

They passed several arrangements, corner groupings, where three-tiered coffee tables seemed randomly placed as though the decorator had lacked decision. Adam stopped and pointed to a floral arrangements in a clear glass bowl. Undoubtedly a florist frog or a piece of styrofoam lurked somewhere in the bottom and held arrangements in place, but it was completely hidden by the hundreds of clear glass marbles that half filled the dish.

'Perfect party toy,' Adam said. Imagine this. You have thirty people in for a cocktail party. Some careless arm bumps the table—and the marbles spill——'

The vision of those marbles cascading across a multi-tiered table and bouncing on the floor with the attendant results caused Janet to giggle.

Ten feet away a salesman, industriously writing out a sales ticket for a customer, turned and glared in their direction.

'Let's move on,' Janet said hastily. 'I'm beginning to understand why you're not a burglar. Your talent is inciting riots.'

They hurried across the huge showroom in the direction of free-standing dividers that beckoned shelter from the disapproving stare of the salesclerk. Janet, leading the way, walked into the boudoir section before she'd realised it. She wasn't ready to look at bedroom furniture. And particularly not with Adam present. He'd shortly be out of her life, and she could visualise many lonely nights ahead. The last thing she wanted was the memory of him standing by a dresser or a bed that she later bought. The fewer associations in her life, the better.

The first room arrangement was cream and gold. The headboard of the bed, the night stands, the dressers, all carried a strong motif of horizontal gold striping. Even the painting over the bed was a series of lines running parallel with the ceiling and the floor.

'I'd say we'd better lie down and not mess up the arrangement,' murmured Adam, the lowering of his eyelids matching the suggestive tone of his voice.

'I'd say we should stand up and move on to a room with more vertical décor,' Janet countered, and suited actions to words.

But her desire to remove them from suggestive surroundings was thwarted by her direction. Behind the next set of dividers they discovered the sensuality of black. The soft gleam of the satin finish on the plain black massive furniture was enhanced by the mind-numbing depths of a black velvet spread on the bed. The decorator had chosen to use accessories of varying depths of purple in the lamps, dresser accessories and wall hangings. Janet's mind rebelled at the mental sound of black and purple. But she felt herself drawn to the visual sensuality of the combination.

'Mmmm,' Adam gave his approval. 'Buy your fantasy and have it delivered on Monday.'

Though he was no closer to her than he had been throughout their entire shopping experience, Janet was suddenly totally aware of the man behind her. The bulwarks she had been trying to build were being stripped away by the suggestions offered in the depths of that velvet spread.

'For that bed, a woman should wear a black négligé,' Adam said softly. 'Long, I think. Like a cloudy veil, as if she was just emerging from his dreams.'

His voice was soft, husky. Janet could envisage lying on that bed, sunk in the depths of that velvet spread. The paleness of her skin, dusky beneath the illusion of sheer black négligé as though emerging out of the darkness of loneliness, moving into the light of desire and fulfilment. Her imagination brought a weakening of her knees and a ragged breath escaped her lips, bringing her back to reality with a jerk.

'Black velvet would show lint,' she snapped, and hurried through the opening that led back into the main showrooms and the safer area of the dining-room ensembles.

'Who'd notice lint?' Adam asked as he followed her.

Janet continued to search for a path between the arrangement of furniture. 'As my grandmother used to say, black picks up everything but men and money.' As soon as she'd spoken she knew—she should have left Grandmother's saying in Iowa.

'I won't vouch for the money,' Adam said, 'but your grandmother——'

'Never mind!' Janet found the main aisle leading to the side door and increased her speed. 'I've had enough of modern furniture.'

She was glad to escape from the store and stand in the comparative dimness of the parking lot. The evening breeze helped to cool the temperature of her senses. Mercifully, Adam stood some four feet away. She felt as if she'd be unable to cope with any closer proximity. But his attitute was making her nervous. The knowing look creeping out of his half-veiled expression was driving her to seek an escape. If he was walking out of her life, she wouldn't allow him to take with him the knowledge of how she felt.

'I think I've seen enough furniture,' she said. 'I'm not getting a true picture of what I want. I need to go home and think about it.'

She wasn't sure why that remark caused Adam's brows to lower in a sudden frown.

He stood for a moment, jangling his keys as if he was

caught in some indecision, and then brightened. 'I bet I know just the place for you.'

'You're kidding.' Norman looked at Rhoda across the small table. The cocktail lounge was so dim he could hardly see her.

'I'm not kidding. And if you breathe a word of this I'll——' Rhoda paused, thinking of the most terrible punishment she could conjure. 'I'll spill a cup of coffee on your new drawings!'

'I'm not worried about you.' Norman was contemptuous of her threat. 'If I let this out, the boss would do worse than you can.' He stared down at the blue pamplet he held close to the shaded candle on the table. 'That's one brave woman.'

'And he's in love with her,' Rhoda said.

'No.' Norman disagreed. 'She's not his type. He likes party girls—fun for the evening and no trouble when he's busy.'

'He doesn't marry his party girls,' Rhoda said.

'He's not marrying this one either. If she's the one he was mad at on Thursday, he's more likely to kill her.'

'That's what convinced me,' Rhoda nodded triumphantly. 'Wait until you fall in love, you'll see.'

Norman picked up the pamphlet again and stared at it. 'If any of our clients were to see this——'

'Don't think about it!' Rhoda shuddered.

Norman put the folded flyer down and took another sip of his drink. 'What do you have in mind?'

'I don't know.'

'Then why did you call me? I was watching a movie on television——'

'To help me develop an idea. There must be something we can do.'

'Forget it. You'll get clobbered, meddling in his business. Leave me out of it.'

'You want to go through months like the past few days?'

Norman shrugged. 'At least he's not mad at us—not yet.'

'But he won't be,' Rhoda argued. 'If we play our cards right, he won't know we are involved.'

'I still say you're heading for a hanging.'

'He won't *know*,' Rhoda insisted. 'Let's see. What do we have to work with?'

Norman finished his drink and pushed the glass to the side. 'Two people who are totally out of their minds and two people——' with a brush of his hand he indicated himself and Rhoda '—who are just as bad.'

'Okay, then we'll live with months like last Thurday, Friday, and today. I tell you he's in love with her, and he won't get over it in a week.'

That silenced Norman for a minute. He sighed the surrender of his objections.

'Okay, let's see, we've got two people——'

'We established that! Now how do we get them together?' Rhoda demanded.

'With extreme care.'

'Norman!'

'What do you want from me? They're not going to get together unless it's to kill each other. I can't see how we can get her into the office,' Norman stated the obvious.

'Or send him to the halfway house where she works.'

'Or get her to his apartment.'

'Or him to Harry's house.'

'Or him to Harry's?' Norman brightened. 'Maybe we *could* send him to Harry's.'

'How?' Rhoda emptied her glass and signalled for another round of drinks. 'He went the first time because he needed a set of plans, only we have all the jobs in the office——'

'But if some of them were at Harry's——' He let the

idea hang in mid-air, waiting for Rhoda to pick it up.

'You mean breaking in again, don't you?'

Norman grinned. 'I saw how he opened that window.' He pulled a small scrap of paper from his pocket. 'Let's see. He hasn't looked at every job since he's been back. What are we working with in the next few days? If he hasn't looked at them, he wouldn't know whether they were at Harry's or not.'

'There's Patterson's job. That has to go on Wednesday. Then Sunnyside Acres is a good bet. We should pick up the preliminary check from the county before the end of the week. We'll need the original plans on that——'

'Bent Willows is up for review on Thurdsay,' Rhoda added. 'We'll need the originals to make ten sets of prints.' She frowned. 'That one won't do. Why would Harry have taken an engineering project home?'

Norman frowned, then shrugged and smiled slyly. 'Who can tell anything about Harry? The main thing is to get the plans into that house. Then he'll have to go after them.'

'It won't work,' Rhoda sighed. 'He'll just tell us to call her.'

Norman threw his companion a look of contempt. 'Haven't you ever transposed a number when you were dialling? Who says we have to reach her?'

She leaned forward to see the cryptic notes he had made. 'I'm afraid of this.'

'You dragged me out here and you didn't come up with an idea!'

'I know,' Rhoda admitted, committing herself. 'So the next question is when? For the sake of the company, the sooner the better.' She picked up her second drink and finished it. 'The third question is, can we get in the house at night again?'

'You know, I had a friend who worked in one of those

halfway houses. He worked odd shifts.'

'Then maybe we'd better call,' said Rhoda. 'We'll go the first night the phone doesn't answer.'

She took a dime from her purse and threaded her way between the tables towards the sign that said rest rooms and telephone. In two minutes she was back. 'We're going the first night the phone doesn't answer?'

'Yep,' Norman replied fast enough, though his tone seemed reluctant.

'Then we might as well get it over with,' she said. 'She must be working tonight. Let's go burgling.'

An hour and a half later, Norman parked his car round the corner from Harry's house and gathered up several rolls of drawings. Rhoda scrambled out of the passenger door carrying two more sets as they hurried down the alley.

When they reached the window of the Binns' house, Norman struggled with the catch. As Adam had done, he used a plastic charge card. But obviously he misunderstood the trick. Then Rhoda's impatience took over. She dug a paperclip from her pocket and worked the wire underneath the catch until it clicked. 'It takes just the right touch,' she whispered triumphantly. 'A touch of larceny. Beg your pardon—burglary.'

Norman climbed in the window and Rhoda, standing outside, saw the faint glow of his penlight flash round the room. The light went out and he pushed the curtains aside again. 'Hand them in one at a time. I'll store them in Harry's bin, so that she won't notice.'

Rhoda was just handing him the first set of plans when——

'Freeze! Police!'

Janet sat primly on her side of the car as Adam drove from the furniture store and a few minutes later pulled into the parking lot of a small shopping centre. She'd been half-afraid he'd take her home as she'd requested, but his destination had been another store.

'Where are we going?' she asked.

'To a place I think you'll like. An idea place.'

Janet was surprised when he opened the glass door for her. Her nose was assailed with the dusky adours of wicker, candles and incense. Glass and brass and straw, paper fans and lanterns, rattan and wicker furniture, baskets, Indian prints and Chinese silks all seemed to be struggling for space and crowding into narrow aisles. To Janet, it was a wonderland of the exotic, a safari through the memoirs of imagined adventures.

As Adam had said, it was an idea place.

In the furniture stores she had looked at the couches and the sofas, the dining-room sets, the occasional chairs, the end tables and coffee tables, and had not been able to visualise any of them in the carriage house. But as she raised her eyes to the ceiling of this shop, her attention was caught by a round white paper lantern, three feet in diameter. She had no trouble at all visualising it hanging in the carriage house.

'Oh, I want one of those,' she said. And despite her high heels she raised herself on tiptoe, as if the additional inch of height would bring her close to the lantern, some ten feet above her head. 'Now I know what I want. *Tall* things.'

'Tall things,' Adam echoed, his eyes laughing at her. 'There's a tall thing. Don't know what it is.' He pointed across the room, where a chain descending from the ceiling supported a fabric that hung tentlike over a round wooden ring and descended out of sight beyond a row of display shelves. When they found a circuitous path between the stacks of chairs and shelves of dishes, glasses and candlesticks, they discovered a nylon mosquito net artistically draped round a small sofa. Janet stood staring at it for a moment, and in a burst of imaginative ideas she picked up a box from the stack beside the display. She clutched it to her bosom, knowing she might be wasting her money, but the tall net spoke to her.

'Tall plants,' she said, suddenly seeing one standing between the high windows of the living-room in the carriage house.

'They don't grow out of mosquito netting,' Adam cautioned her.

'No, no,' she said, slightly impatient. 'Hanging plants. Tall plants. That's what the living-room of the carriage house needs, and this.' She carried the mosquito net as she walked along, her ideas suddenly coming into focus. 'And I've always wanted one of these chairs.' She stopped by the tall wicker Bali chair, surveyed the round fan back and the graceful curved arms, and with a sudden decision parked the mosquito net in the chair. She was seeing brass and greenery and wicker as if she were viewing a decorating scheme in a magazine.

'Don't forget the big lantern,' Adam reminded her.

'Oh! Where were they?'

'Over in the corner. If you're serious, I'll get you one.'

'Oh, I'm serious,' Janet said.

When he walked away, she stood wondering at this sudden spurt of what might be wasteful spending, but she had been looking for days, and each day she'd grown more despondent because she couldn't make a decision. At least she'd made a start. She gazed at the wonderland of exotic items and suddenly spotted a childhood dream come true.

Over in the corner stood a wicker giraffe, fully five feet high.

'Idiotic,' she told herself as her feet took two steps in that direction. She backed away, remaining by the Bali chair, and stared at the giraffe. There were times in a person's life, she told herself, when one threw caution to the wind, when some silly something, an inconsequential, unnecessary item seemed to bring the rest of the world in focus. And for Janet that giraffe was like an arrow, pointing the way to solving her decorating problems. She could see him standing on the balconied hall of the second floor of the carriage house, and suddenly everything she wanted for the apartment came into focus.

She didn't need to buy him, she thought, but when she took her eyes away from the silly creature all her visions dimmed. They dimmed because he belonged on that balcony, she decided, and, squaring her shoulders, she marched over and picked him up before she could change her mind.

A silly stupid giraffe. She could imagine Adam laughing at her. But he was *her* giraffe and he was going home with her.

Before she could change her mind, she carried Alfred, as she had decided to call him, over to the counter. The salesgirl was busy writing up Janet's purchases when Adam returned with the lantern. Janet's cheque-book was already out, and she hurriedly paid for her purchases before her nerve gave way. She had succumbed to the California influence, she decided, but she was going to do strange and wonderful things with her apartment.

'Well now, let's see,' said Adam. 'You have a Bali chair, a mosquito net to put over a bed you don't have, a paper lantern without a light fixture, and a straw giraffe.'

'Wicker,' Janet corrected him.

'Wicker,' he said. 'All the necessities of life.'

She refused to be daunted. 'It's a beginning,' she said obstinately, her spirit still soaring until the salesgirl brought her forcibly down to earth.

'Do you need some help getting these things to the car?'

Janet stood, mouth agape, as Adam grinned at her. 'Oh, no.' she said. 'Oh, I'm so sorry. I hadn't thought about the fact that we were in *your* car.'

'Think nothing of it,' he teased. 'We can get the chair in the trunk and tie it down, or we can go back to Harry's and get your car.'

They opted to go for her car, and back at the store they loaded Janet's purchases into it. She followed Adam to her new apartment where they took the chair and the giraffe from her car and other items from his coupé.

When she had closed and locked the carriage house again they stood in the moonlight by the cars, both silent and uncomfortable. Adam had lost his decisiveness again, and Janet stood frozen, afraid to move, for fear he might offer her his last goodbye. Finally she couldn't stand the silence any longer.

'I'm sorry I put you to so much trouble. I just got carried away and didn't think,' she said.

He stood looking out into the dark shrubbery. He didn't turn as he spoke.

'How about making it up to me——'

As his pause lengthened into the uncomfortable, Janet swallowed and dared a question.

'What do you mean?'

'We've solved part of your problem, how about taking a look at my place?'

She took a breath and offered up a small thanks, but she wondered if she was facing another temporary reprieve, building a hope that had no chance of success. Still, she couldn't help clutching at another opportunity, no matter how slim.

'Okay, I'll follow you in my car.'

As they drove along the city streets, her hands on the

steering wheel were trembling. They were going to his apartment, and she couldn't decide whether to be happy or scared.

CHAPTER NINE

JANET had been afraid to go to Adam's apartment, and on the way she had tried to clarify her feelings. She attempted to place the blame on her mid-Western upbringing, but the fear refused to rest there. Nor was she afraid of Adam Richfield.

She tried to put a name to her feeling as they entered a huge old Spanish-style apartment building. The sophisticated security system, the subdued gleam of polished floors, the shining brass wall sconces and old-fashioned hall runners alerted her to the quality of the building. Behind the widely spaced doors with the discreet apartment numbers were some of the more élite apartment dwellers of the area.

But it wasn't until he had led her down the hall and opened the last door on the right that Janet understood her reluctance to accompany him to his apartment. Though she had refused to give it a label, her fear had been discovering a need in Adam that she could fill, which would make it even harder on her when he said goodbye. Though she'd no preconceived opinion of what his home would be like, she wasn't surprised, though she was immediately struck by its size. They entered a short hall from which a stairway rose to the second floor, and ahead she could see a large living-room. The ceiling was high, in the old-fashioned style. The ornate wainscoting and ceiling moulding whispered quality from another era.

Clearly Adam understood quality and balance. The soft gleam of the leather-upholstered couch and chairs, the well-proportioned end tables and old brass lamps were well placed. The Spartan quality kept the room cold.

Obviously no woman had added a softening touch. Janet was both relieved and frightened by the discovery. Certainly some female would have wanted to put a plant on the side-table, giving the room a touch of life, lay a magazine on the leather-topped coffee table or turn the large chair near the window so that it faced the couch in a more companionable atmosphere. The room was neat, but as impersonal as the furniture store showroom.

As Janet moved across the expanse of soft carpeting, she saw where Adam 'lived'. In the large dining-room a desk backed up against the wall, and spread across a beautiful pecan dining-room table was a thick layer of felt covered by a pale green sheet of thick vinyl. Almost hidden under the rolls of plans was a small computer and the assorted paraphernalia of an engineer.

'The southern branch office of Associated Architects and Engineers?' asked Janet.

'North-eastern,' Adam shrugged. 'That's not much to clear away if I have company in. How about a drink?'

'Make it tea,' she said.

He'd turned towards the bar, a beautiful old cabinet whose purpose she only recognised because it stood slightly away from the wall. But at her restriction on the liquid refreshment he looked back at her, his eyes ambiguous.

'Seriously, if we're going to consider your decorating problems, we ought to do it with a clear head,' Janet explained, and then turned back to look at the tall-backed chairs that matched the dining-room table.

She was both relieved and disappointed. He did need help with the apartment. She shrugged away that feeling of loss, and asked herself why she'd expected his invitation to his apartment to be a seduction. They'd agreed to be honest, hadn't they? What did she want? More silly games and lies? Lies, somehow, seemed like a harsh word. But teasing, harassment, those terms didn't fit. No, she wanted honesty. Damn it, she just didn't want it as impersonally as Adam Richfield was willing to offer it.

In the kitchen she heard his footsteps moving about, a soft hollow sound of leather soles on tile-covered wood floors. Her feet wanted to keep moving too. She pushed two rolls of drawings aside and laid her handbag on the edge of the dining-room table.

'Do I explore the rest of the apartment on my own or wait for the grand tour?' she called, trying to make her voice gay and light.

'Exploring is always more fun,' Adam said, his words punctuated by a light squeak in a cabinet door.

Back in the dining-room Janet nodded, thinking she probably had no right to expect anything else, recrossed the living-room into the hall and ascended the carpeted steps. She resolutely pulled her mind off Adam, continued up to the second floor, and went in the various rooms she found.

He certainly was neat, she thought, and for someone who worked in his dining-room he had a lot of free space upstairs. Two of the bedrooms were completely furnished, but had it not been for a set of brushes on a bureau and a dresser caddy for holding keys and wallets, Janet would not have known which was his bedroom.

The smaller doors she dismissed as bathrooms or closets. The third room was as empty and bare as if the apartment had been completely vacant.

To Janet the bedrooms were like the living-room below. Perfectly neat and clean and holding all the personality of a hotel. Good-quality furnishing required a touch of softness to give them a homelike feeling. Adam's apartment wasn't a home. She returned to the living-room as Adam came from the kitchen with a well-laden tea tray.

'What's the verdict?' he asked as he concentrated on lowering the tray to the coffee table.

Janet took a seat at the end of the couch and watched while he filled the cups. He'd removed his jacket and tie, she noticed. The dark curling hair peeped from between the open collar in wayward little curls.

'You certainly run a neat hotel. Your housekeeping puts mine to shame,' she said.

'I'll give you her name. She comes in twice a week——' His chin jerked up. 'What do you mean, hotel?'

'I'm sorry.' Janet was pleased to get an emotional rise out of him. 'But that's what you have.' She looked round again at the preciseness of the furniture. 'I have the feeling you pulled out your slide rule and calculated where the furniture should go.'

'Don't be ridiculous. Slide rules are as out of date as Model T Fords.' His quick defence caused Janet to smile.

If her description of his furniture placement was over-precise, at least he'd stepped it off. The balance was too perfect. He'd measured it as carefully as he'd locate a building on a lot.

'What's wrong with where I put the furniture?' Adam looked round as if seeing the room for the first time.

'Nothing,' said Janet. 'It's a beautiful start.' Her words carried the conviction of honesty. 'I can see that you and I work from opposite directions.'

'Oh?'

Janet nodded, her eyes brimming. 'You started with the essentials.'

Adam's eyes lit up. 'And you started with a giraffe.'

'And a mosquito net.'

'You're saying I stopped before I got to my mosquito

net,' he nodded. His eyes were serious for a bit, and then a twinkle started. 'Where do you suggest I put one?'

His tone had been light, but suddenly Janet had the uncomfortable feeling that she was being tested. 'Upstairs in the empty room,' she said promptly. 'You hang it above the new drafting table and pull it closed to keep the dust off the plans.' As she spoke she laid her arm on the back of the sofa and pointed to the clutter on the dining-room table.

'That's a long way from the coffee pot,' Adam complained.

'Nevertheless, upstairs with the clutter,' Janet used a schoolmarmish voice.

He picked up his tea, took a sip, looked in it for a moment as though he was stalling for time, and then put it back on the table. Tucking one leg under him, he turned slightly from his end of the sofa to face Janet. Waiting and speculation filled his face. 'Go on. Now that I have a neat dining-room—an extension of the hotel—what next?'

The light question showed that her first remark still rankled slightly. She was still bothered with the feeling of being tested. His face was partially in repose, though lurking in his eyes she sensed, rather than saw, a defensiveness, as though he felt a need to protect something as personal as his home.

'Well, from there it's harder,' she said slowly. 'You see, it depends entirely on what you want to do with it.'

Her words caused him to pause. He looked a little startled. 'Do with it? What do you do with it? You live in it.'

'But you don't,' Janet said, flicking her fingers to indicate the perfectly neat room. 'People have "hobbies".' Across the room she saw the television. 'They watch TV. Where's your programme listing?'

Adam frowned, opened a drawer in the end table and

picked up a thin magazine, the type that came out of the local Sunday paper. He dropped it on the coffee table by the tray. 'That better? Maybe I should stand my fishing rods in that corner and my golf clubs over there.'

'That's not what I meant.'

'I should start building model planes and get glue all over the tables, huh?'

Janet was miserable. She wasn't explaining herself well and she wanted to make her meaning clear. In a day or so Adam would probably be out of her life and she'd be out of his. She was beginning to accept the inevitable, but somehow she wanted to leave a mark. Something to show she'd been a part of his time and attention for a little while. Just to be forgotten seemed such a cheat.

That's ego, she reminded herself. So, it was ego. She still wanted to be remembered.

'I think I'd hate glue on these tables,' she said. She was searching for a way to take the wariness out of his eyes. To dissolve the defensiveness that might stop him accepting any valid point she might make. 'You'll think I'm silly,' she said slowly, 'but you don't have any castles——'

That was a stupid way to begin. He'd think she was crazy. She'd never get her meaning across like that. She stared into the empty fireplace and wondered how it could have escaped her attention until that moment. She struggled to bring back what she was trying to say.

'This room lacks dreams,' she said. 'There's nothing in it to say you want anything other than to watch the evening news.' Her eyes flickered in his direction.

She was surprised by his arrested look. He was concentrating hard on her meaning. She took courage and continued.

'Close your eyes and think. What do you want out of your life? Part of it should take place in this room. It should reflect your goals. Your lifestyle should help you grow—at least, that's what *I* think a home should be.'

Adam's eyes remained open, but he focused on the blank wall to Janet's right. His gaze flickered back to her for a moment and then returned to the wall. 'What does anyone want?' he murmured. He seemed to be speaking more to himself than to her. 'Success, I suppose. Love? I suppose—in a home—I guess comfort after a day's work.' He moved slightly, as though his energy had been directed into his thinking and he was warming to his subject. 'The visible rewards of the day's work that help to make the next day easier to face.'

'That's a beautiful thought.' Janet broke in, admiring his depth of insight once he truly became interested in the subject.

Along with her appreciation of his thinking came a sense of loss. She'd had no idea he had such a deep personal awareness. Their association until that time had been so shallow.

'I think you've found your own answer,' she said. Her emotional deflation came from knowing that he only needed his purpose awakened. From that point he wouldn't require her assistance.

'Think about it,' she said. 'What do you think the room needs to show your success and help you to achieve more?' She stopped. He's also mentioned love. She wasn't willingly opening the door on that subject.

'You're leaving this to me, aren't you?' He seemed dissatisfied, as though she wasn't keeping her part of the bargain.

But her counselling training had taken over.

'Try my way first,' she held to her decision.

'Okay, I'll think about it.' His tone carried a strong man's disappointment. Not quite plaintive, a little irritated. Slightly resigned, as if he found himself forced to take an unexpected and unwelcome job. 'Maybe you're right. If all the choices are made by one person, then the room has the personality of its owner.' That seemed to give him pause. He, too, stared into the fireplace, then he turned and stretched his long legs in front of him, his feet pushing at the rug until waves of fabric rose in front of his pressing heels.

'But a slavish attempt to make the room fit me and me alone is self-defeating, I think.'

'How?'

'Because I don't want to live in this room alone,' he said slowly. 'Some time, with the right person, I want to share it.'

Life just wasn't fair! Janet thought. She had found it terribly difficult to help him in his personal escort endeavours before she knew she was in love with him. Now to help him plan his life in order to bring another woman into it was just too much. *Oh, just let me out of here,* she silently begged the fates.

But Adam was beginning to talk. 'If I want a woman in this room, I have to make *her* feel welcome,' he mused more to himself than to Janet. 'I want it to be uncluttered, to give the feeling of space,' he paused, folded his hands behind his head as he gazed up at the ceiling. 'She mustn't feel trapped.' He moved again, drawing his right leg under him. He straightened and turned to face her again, leaving the space of a wide leather cushion between them though his gaze held hers as securely as if she'd been bound.

'You can't trap caring and affection as if they were wild animals,' he paused, waiting for an answer from her.

Janet's heart spoke all the answers, but she dared not use them. She strove for something neutral.

'You have the space. She can run round the furniture if she wants to,' she replied, and because his look was giving her the feeling of the entrapment he denied she turned, placing her feet primly side by side on the floor in front of her. Glancing back at him she saw the twinkle of mischief in his eyes. Darn him, he'd read her movements with an accuracy that brought colour to her cheeks.

'It's my job to keep her from wanting to run,' he said. His voice had suddenly changed. His words were smooth, his tone well modulated with that indefinable quality she'd heard when he was allowing her to believe he was a criminal. Her pride rose on its hind legs and demanded she should give him back trick for trick. She turned round to face him, curling her feet as she laid her left arm on the back of the sofa and supported her chin in her hand. He wasn't making a fool of her again.

'And how are you going to prevent her if she doesn't want to stay?'

'By making her feel appreciated,' Adam said softly. 'By providing the things a woman wants.'

'Oh?' Being with him should be enough, she thought, but she wouldn't tell him that.

'Women like softness, I think,' he said, rising from the sofa.

'In their men?' Janet asked, determined to throw him off stride.

'I was speaking of atmosphere,' he answered, his smoothness unimpared by her thrust. He turned down the lamps, moving round the room until he'd made a complete circle. 'And they like a feeling of warmth.' He knelt at the fireplace, and drawing a match from a long box he lit the logs, holding the match far beneath the stack. Janet assumed, by the continued burning, that he must have carefully arranged the starter kindling. 'And music.' He rose from the fireplace and strolled to a closet. Almost at once the soft strains of Mendelssohn seemed to come from all round the room.

'Very nice.' Janet, caught by her heart, would have

liked to breathe into that comment all her approval of
the atmosphere and the company, but pride demanded
she should give him a leveller of bracing impersonality,
as though she was a spectator at a dog show. 'But I
wonder,' she added, 'if you really want to make use of
that fire, shouldn't you have some cushions on the floor
or a bearskin rug?'

'You're kidding! I think bearskins went out of date
with Fitzgerald. And it would be a bit obvious, wouldn't
it?'

You bet, Janet thought. 'Not at all,' she answered.
She could just imagine some female reactions—other
women probably wouldn't mind. But Adam probably
knew plenty of the latter, and he was still living alone.

'No, I think a little more subtlety,' he said softly as he
returned to the sofa. 'A good dinner, a good wine.' He
poured more tea into her cup and handed it to her.

The grace with which he leaned forward, the glow of
the reflected firelight in his eyes, and the ambiguous
smile curling his lips, caused her heart to flutter, and the
dark brew seemed heady as champagne.

As he picked up his own cup, he settled on the centre
cushion of the sofa and turned to face her. The light
played on the planes of his face, accentuating the
masculinity of his features. The flames reflected in his
eyes seemed to be burning within him, and threatened
Janet's strongly controlled emotions like a torch thrown
among dry leaves.

She dropped her gaze to her cup, trying to pull back
the impersonal tone her pride demanded. But somehow
she could find no words to fit a tone of light comment.

'When I bring the right woman in my home, I don't
want her to think I'm looking for sex alone,' Adam said,
putting his cup down and leaning his right side against
the back of the sofa.

His arm dropped gently across the back cushions,

reaching beyond her shoulder, but not touching her. He paused as if waiting for her to speak, but her tongue was imprisoned between the war of her heart and her pride.

'It's important that she know I like the way the light plays on her hair. The way she curls up on a cushion, like a kitten ready for a nap. I want her to know I value what she thinks, that I could spend a lifetime just looking into her face and watching the changes of expression.'

Janet felt as if she'd explode with conflicting emotions. He'd paused again as if waiting for her to speak, but her tongue refused.

'You see, I can't complete this place alone,' Adam went on when she didn't answer. 'There has to be some of her in it too. It's the way of life when two people share it. They each provide a different set of values and weave them together.'

Janet nodded, still not trusting her tongue.

'I provide the basics,' Adam's hand waved to include the room. 'And she brings the giraffe.'

Again she nodded. He was right. His background, his way of thinking, would cause him to lean towards essentials. And while he might enjoy the frivolous, his mind would be impatient with the choosing and the implementing of folderols that made life softer and a more interesting experience.

The giraffe!

Her eyelids fluttered with surprise as she realised he was waiting for her to speak. And this time he wasn't filling her silence for her.

She tried to look up, to assess the expression on his face. But as eyes with pupils widened by darkness shy and turn from the light, so her gaze kept pulling away from his searching look. His voice had lost the smoothness, but she couldn't remember when. She was aware of the curious vulnerability in him. It was so foreign to her opinion of him that she wasn't sure if she read it correctly. What did she say? Did his reference to the giraffe indicate a proposal?

Oh, God! What should she do? He'd pulled so many tricks. Was he teasing her again? Why hadn't he made himself plainer if he was making a declaration?

She stared down into her teacup again. The blackness was a void sucking her into its depths. If she blew this chance, he'd probably take her home and she'd never see him again. If she accepted that ambiguous proposal and he didn't mean it——

He was drawing away, reaching for the teacup. He picked it up and put it back impatiently on the table. The vulnerable look had disappeared. His chin line had hardened. Say *some*thing! Janet commanded herself, but he was turning away, the time for her answer had passed.

They were both startled by the ringing of the telephone. Adam, who sat staring into the fire, jerked his head round as if the instrument were some alien thing that had somehow slipped in while his attention was elsewhere. Janet felt the bell was a strident period put on their conversation and any further chance to salvage their relationship.

The phone brought out anger in him. He jerked upright, then leaned over to pick up the tray from the coffee table.

'You answer it,' he snapped. 'If it's for the escort service, *you* handle it!'

She moved to the other end of the sofa and picked up the telephone in the middle of its third ring.

'Adam Richfield's residence,' she said.

The voice on the end of the phone was feminine and seductive. 'Is this the Richfield Escort Service?' it asked.

Janet almost dropped the phone.

All the tricks and games rolled back on her in a suffocating wave. Back with it came the game Adam had played on her that night. If it was a game. The pain, the fear that he'd been teasing returned. She'd never had an opportunity to answer him, to find out the truth. But the fates had given her another opportunity. When she answered the telephone caller, her voice was surprisingly steady and clear.

'I'm sorry, the escort service is closed. Mr Richfield is under exclusive contract.'

As she lowered the receiver back to its cradle she heard dimly the low laugh coming over the wire. She'd taken a big step, but once it was made she couldn't turn and face him. She walked over to the fireplace and stared into the fire; her heart seemed to be leaping in time with the flames.

While she'd been on the phone he'd walked across the room towards the kitchen, but as she gazed into the fireplace she heard the rattle of paper and cups as he put the tray on the dining-room table. His leather soles on the carpet whispered his approach. She felt his hands as they came to rest on her shoulders. His voice was husky, and not much louder than his footsteps.

'Does that mean I'm going to be fully rehabilitated? It's a full-time job, you know.'

'I guess if anyone ever needed it, you do.' Janet answered, wishing he'd speak plainly, but while her logic argued her heart laughed at the doubts. It insisted she should understand. She was just turning to face him when someone pounded on the door of the apartment.

'Damn!' Adam jumped with the disorientation of being jerked out of deep thought. He strode towards the hallway, his heels tapping a rhythm of impatience.

Janet went back to the sofa, turned up the lamp and sat waiting. She looked over her shoulder, watching as he opened the door to face two people who looked vaguely familiar, and two uniformed police officers.

Though Adam's back was to her, she could read his surprise and speculation in his change of stance. His head drew back slightly and turned sideways a fraction. He didn't speak as he stood aside, and with a wave of his hand signalled to the four people to enter the apartment. The short stout woman who led the way walked the length of the hall and into the living-room before seeing Janet. She came to a standstill and gave her companion a speaking look that caused Janet to wonder what was going on.

Adam had closed the door and entered behind the second policeman, who carried several rolls of large paper. Janet was, by now, familiar enough with architectural and engineering prints to recognise what he held. Adam gave the rolls only a cursory glance before he turned on the short woman, who was dressed in dark clothes.

'Okay, Rhoda, what have you been up to?'

'I'm pleading the Fifth,' she said with a quick look in Janet's direction.

'Norman?' Adam turned his head to stare at Rhoda's companion, but the slight blond man had suddenly developed an all-absorbing interest in the carpet.

Derek turned back to the officers.

'We caught them breaking into a house over on Bayview Drive——'

Harry Binns' house was on Bayview Drive.

'We would have booked them,' said the tall slim officer who was holding the plans, 'but they weren't robbing the house. They were putting these into it.' He indicated the drawings.

'And they had quite a story to tell,' the shorter one added. His glance shifted towards Janet and then back at Adam.

All the elation Janet had felt crashed round her, the

pain of the thud carrying the force of a plummet from the heights. Rhoda and Norman had been putting the plans into the house, and the only reason could be to cause Adam to return for them. If he had to be tricked into returning, then he had no intention of coming just to see her.

She couldn't decide whether he had been playing another game with her or if she had created meanings out of her hope, not from what he'd actually said. He hadn't made any secret out of coming to Harry's to say goodbye. How the visit could have stretched into a shopping trip was a mystery to her. She was a fool to think his ambiguous statements had been a proposal.

She needed to get away from Adam Richfield. Suddenly she was on her feet, hurrying to the dining-room to get her handbag, and before anyone noticed she was past them and heading for the door.

'Janet?' Adam called after her, but she didn't stop. She heard his urgent murmur as she opened the door and started down the hall. Before she reached the outside entrance, she heard quick footsteps. His hand closed on her arm, bringing her to a halt.

'Wait a minute—come back! Let me straighten this out——'

'I think it's clear enough,' Janet said, refusing to look at him. 'Thank your friends Rhoda and Norman for their good intentions.'

'Rhoda and Norman are idiots. What they meant to do——'

'They meant to trick you into coming back, which means you weren't planning to come on your own. *Now let me go!*'

Janet jerked her arm away and, still not looking at him, ran from the building and out into the street.

She drove home in a stupor of pain. Automatically she prepared for bed, her hands going through the motions of her evening ablutions, finding her pyjamas and turning back the bed coverings. Lying in the dark, she stared up at the ceiling, or where she supposed it would be. Her eyes wouldn't close but her brain seemed comatose, refusing to think for fear the activation of a grey cell would bring on the suffering that would sooner or later envelop her.

She had no idea how long she remained in that state when she was roused by an unidentifiable sound coming from the general area of the den. She listened to the *plop-thud*, and after the third she pushed back the covers and climbed out of bed, thinking she'd left a window open, and the breeze was probably blowing the curtains against a table. She had visions of a lamp rocking as it was pushed by the curtains, and if the breeze strengthened it could be knocked over.

As she entered the room and flipped on the light she saw the open window, but the curtain wasn't creating a problem. She stood perfectly still, staring at Adam, standing outside, blinking at the bright light and ducking out of sight. His head appeared again and he threw a roll of plans into the room. They fell among several other sets with a *plop-thud*. Though he must know she was there, he didn't look at her. He bent, picked up another set and threw them in.

'What are you doing?' Janet demanded when she found her voice. She should have realised that any sounds coming from the den at night must come from Adam or his associates, but her mind had refused to consider the possibility, afraid of another false hope. Now she stood, still trying to maintain that protective numbness, but despite all her efforts it was draining away.

She knew Adam heard her, but he kept bending down, reappearing, throwing other rolls in the window.

'What are you doing?' she demanded again.

'I'm proving that if I need an excuse to come back again, I can set it up myself,' he said, continuing to toss the drawings on the floor of the den.

Janet crossed the room, stepping over the clutter of rolls, and almost made it to the window. Adam, who had bent to pick up another bundle and hadn't seen her appear threw it in, unintentionally tossing it into her path. Janet dodged the roll and stumbled. He leaned in and thrust out an arm, his reach just adequate to catch her shoulder and steady her. Then he pulled her into his arms. Feeling as if she had just been offered life again, Janet savoured the warmth of his embrace.

When she raised her face he kissed her, his lips transmitting an urgency and a need that clarified all the strange happenings and the ambiguous conversations of the evening. When he allowed her to get her breath, she stepped back and almost stumbled again.

'You certainly made a mess on the floor,' she murmured, seeking any comment. Her emotions were too busy soaring to allow a coherent expression of her feelings.

'Can I have the rest of my life to clear it up?' Adam asked, and started to climb in the window.

'Freeze! Police! Oh hell, not *this* bunch again!'

Adam, half in and half out of the window, looked back into the darkness, gave a wave and finished climbing across the sill. By the time his feet touched the floor, the two police officers who had brought Rhoda and Norman to his apartment had moved closer and were illuminated by the light from the den.

'Most houses have doors—didn't anyone ever tell you people about them?' the younger officer asked, trying not to laugh.

'Didn't anyone ever tell you a guy likes to propose to his girl in private?' Adam retorted. 'Or are you here to make it official?'

'Make it official, officer,' demanded Janet. She smiled at Adam. 'But leave him in my custody, I promise to rehabilitate him.'

When the two patrolmen had disappeared from the window, Janet closed and locked it and let the curtains fall back into place. Then she turned to Adam.

'You're going to need a *lot* of rehabilitation,' she warned him.

'Then don't waste another second.'

She stepped into his arms, with the full intention of staying there until the job was completed.

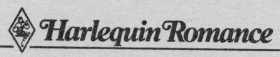

Harlequin Romance

Coming Next Month

Available in November wherever paperback books are sold, or
through Harlequin Reader Service.

In the U.S.
901 Fuhrmann Blvd.
P.O. Box 1397
Buffalo, N.Y. 14240-1397

In Canada
P.O. Box 603
Fort Erie, Ontario
L2A 5X3

What readers say about Harlequin romance fiction...

"I absolutely adore Harlequin romances!
They are fun and relaxing to read, and
each book provides a wonderful escape."
—N.E.,* Pacific Palisades, California

"Harlequin is the best in romantic reading."
—K.G.,* Philadelphia, Pennsylvania

"Harlequins have been my passport to the
world. I have been many places without
ever leaving my doorstep."
—P.Z.,* Belvedere, Illinois

"My praise for the warmth and adventure
your books bring into my life."
—D.F.,*Hicksville, New York

"A pleasant way to relax after a busy day."
—P.W.,* Rector, Arkansas

*Names available on request.

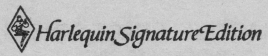
Harlequin Signature Edition

Penny Jordan

Stronger Than Yearning

He was the man of her dreams!

The same dark hair, the same mocking eyes; it was as if the
Regency rake of the portrait, the seducer of Jenna's dream, had
come to life. Jenna, believing the last of the Deverils dead, was
determined to buy the great old Yorkshire Hall—to claim it for
her daughter, Lucy, and put to rest some of the painful memories of Lucy's birth. She had no way of knowing that a direct des-
cendant of the black sheep Deveril even existed—or that James
Allingham and his own powerful yearnings would disrupt her
plan entirely.

Penny Jordan's first Harlequin Signature Edition *Love's Choices* was an
outstanding success. Penny Jordan has written more than 40 best-sell-
ing titles—more than 4 million copies sold.

Now, be sure to buy her latest bestseller, *Stronger Than Yearning*. Available wherever paperbacks are sold—in October.